Anne Fine is a distinguished c[...]
won the Carnegie medal [...]
Children's Award twice, the [...]
Literature Award and a Smarties Prize. An adaptation
of her novel *Goggle-Eyes* has been shown by the BBC
and Twentieth Century Fox filmed her novel *Madame
Doubtfire* as *Mrs Doubtfire*, starring Robin Williams.

Telling Liddy is Anne Fine's fourth adult novel. Her
first, the critically acclaimed *The Killjoy* was also
published by Black Swan: her next, *Taking the Devil's
Advice*, was adapted for radio. her most recent is *In Cold
Domain*. She has two grown-up daughters and lives in
County Durham.

Critical acclaim for *Telling Liddy*:

'An entertaining and revealing account of the complicated emotional structure of an extended family . . . it is also a fine social satire on middle-class life. Fine's observation is sharp, but not cruel, her perspective amused rather than bitter; her account of how wrong things can go when you interfere in someone's life without really understanding your own motives is scarily convincing. She understands people horribly well . . . wrapping interesting characters up in an intriguing plot. You'll read it quickly – and it'll leave you satisfied'
Observer

'There are few writers who so cleverly portray family life and its small joys and desperate torments'
Scotland on Sunday

'Mercilessly funny . . . an intricate plot in which adultery, betrayal and smaller, meaner secrets are revealed'
Mail on Sunday

'Fine's writing is deceptively simple . . . her delicate dissection of ordinary lives is accomplished and, at times, compelling'
Sunday Times

'Fine knows what she wants to do, and has judged precisely what can be stripped away from her prose in order to leave it bare and effective. The explosive, joyous, fantastic imaginativeness of her writing for children is changed here and darkened. *Telling Liddy* is harsh, for all its fluency, and it is a comedy that makes the reader look for the folly in himself. The story takes hold, and won't be shaken off'
Helen Dunmore, *The Times*

'A perspicacious and terrible, wise and embarrassing novel: so much of it shameful, all of it true'
Julie Myerson, *Independent on Sunday*

'A chilling, skilfully constructed novel of family tension and emotional revenge . . . a quiet, unsentimental novel that looks without blinking at the depths to which intelligent, law-abiding people can sink . . . It is uncomfortable to read, but it is full of illuminating insights into human behaviour'
The Times Literary Supplement

TELLING LIDDY

A Sour Comedy

Anne Fine

BLACK SWAN

TELLING LIDDY
A BLACK SWAN BOOK : 0 552 99770 6

Originally published in Great Britain by Bantam Press,
a division of Transworld Publishers Ltd

PRINTING HISTORY
Bantam Press edition published 1998
Black Swan edition published 1999

Set in 11/13pt Garamond 3 by Hewer Text Ltd, Edinburgh

Black Swan Books are published by Transworld Publishers Ltd,
61–62 Uxbridge Road, London W5 5SA,
in Australia by Transworld Publishers (Australia) Pty Ltd,
15–25 Helles Avenue, Moorebank, NSW 2170
and in New Zealand by Transworld Publishers (NZ) Ltd,
3 William Pickering Drive, Albany, Auckland.

Reproduced, printed and bound in Great Britain by
Cox & Wyman Ltd, Reading, Berks.

For A.W., with love and thanks

'I've just had Liddy on the phone,' said Dennis. 'She's in a bloody state, I must say. What on earth have the two of you done to her?'

'We haven't done anything,' said Heather. 'Except tell her.'

TELLING LIDDY

1

BRIDIE PUT HER CUP CAREFULLY BACK ON ITS SAUCER AND stared at her sister across the wide pine table. 'Sorry?'

Nervously Stella repeated, 'So I told Mrs Moffat not to worry, and I'd try to sort it out.'

'No, not that bit,' said Bridie. 'The bit about Ecclefechan.'

'I wanted her to enjoy her holiday,' Stella explained again. 'I didn't see why she should go off worrying. So I told her I'd deal with it.'

'But Mrs Moffat went up to Scotland in *May*.'

Stella's face closed. Stubborn stupidity dropped over it like a portcullis, but ignoring years of professional expertise, Bridie pressed on. 'Do you see what I'm saying, Stella? May! That's nearly three months ago. It's August now.'

'I know it's August.'

Bridie wanted to reach over the table and shake her sister till she rattled. 'So why on earth didn't you tell me?'

'I promised Mrs Moffat I wouldn't say a word to anyone.'

'But that's ridiculous! The woman tells you she thinks your own sister's boyfriend might be a child abuser, and you're not supposed to tell anyone? Not even Liddy herself?'

Stella, she noticed, was studiously ignoring her rising anger, as if that put her on some sort of moral high ground. 'She said she only told me' – and here, astonishingly, Stella paused to give the old conspiratorial grin they'd shared so often about her gossipy cleaning lady's eccentric little turn of phrase – 'because she knew I could be trusted "not to unbutton my beak".'

Two could play at ignoring things. 'So if you weren't to tell anyone, what do you suppose she was expecting you to do?'

She watched her sister's expression revert to careful vacancy. 'I don't know. I'm not sure.'

'Don't be so stupid!' snapped Bridie. 'You must know perfectly well what she expected you to do. She expected you to warn Liddy.'

'Oh, I couldn't do that. Liddy's been so *happy* since George moved in with her.'

'Oh, for heaven's sake!' But it was said weakly, with all the tiredness that suddenly came over Bridie. The drear bone-tiredness of her job. How many times had she heard them in her office, these variations on a theme? 'But they all seemed so happy with him!' 'I didn't want to unsettle everything.' And even, 'I wasn't sure how we'd manage financially without him'. If she could keep her temper through all these stupid, spineless self-deceptions, then she could keep her temper now.

And it was important to keep things in proportion. Nobody knew for a fact that George had done anything to anyone. Ever.

'Tell me again exactly what Mrs Moffat's friend said.'

In her exasperation, Bridie had picked the wrong tone, pitching her sister straight back into sullenness. 'Look, I'm not on trial here. And I'm not one of your customers.'

'Clients.'

'Whatever. Just remember, I didn't have to tell you anything. And I don't like being told off like a naughty girl just because you don't like what you're hearing.'

Bridie tried hard to get a grip. She'd heard the same defensive tone often enough in interviews and coped with it perfectly well. Why was she finding it so difficult to keep her temper now? Was it because it was family, her own niece and nephew at risk? No. If she were honest, it was because she was just itching to slap this sister here, this one in front of her, this stupid, smug, complacent Stella, who traded on her own weakness and lack of spunk, and had been sitting on this information for three whole months and not done a single thing.

'Why didn't you speak to him? Why didn't you just take him aside quietly and tell him what you knew? Then he'd have had to tell Liddy. He'd have thought that at any moment you, or somebody else, might. At least she'd have known, and it would have been up to her. She could have made her own decisions.'

'I couldn't. I promised. Mrs Moffat would kill me.'

This was a line that came up so often at work that Bridie found it almost soothing. 'Look, Stella, it's the only way.

And there's no need to tell him where the information comes from. Anyone in the world could have remembered the case from the papers and passed it on. Mrs Moffat can't be the only person round here with Scottish connections.'

'But he probably didn't do anything anyway. It was "not proven", Mrs Moffat's friend heard.'

' "Not proven" means just that, Stella. Not "not guilty". Just "not proven".'

'You don't know.'

'Neither do you. That's the whole point. It's up to Liddy to make up her mind.'

'Maybe she's made it up already. Have you thought of that? Maybe he's already told her everything Mrs Moffat's told me.'

'Maybe he has. So making sure won't matter, will it?'

She watched her sister's mousy little face close down again. 'I don't know . . .'

'You'd know quickly enough if they were *your* children.'

And that was it. Bridie had gone too far. Stella stood up, and started fussing round her perfect kitchen, glancing at the clock, refolding a tea towel on a rail, pushing a gleaming kettle a few inches to the left, then back again. 'Good heavens! Is it twelve o'clock? I really ought to be getting on with things, if you don't mind, Bridie. There's a couple of phone calls I promised Neil I'd get done before lunchtime.'

Defeated, Bridie rose, and pulled her bag and sweater across the table towards her.

'So what do you want me to do about all this?'

Stella widened her eyes in false innocence.

'Oh, God. Nothing. Nothing at all. I only told you because I couldn't bear the strain of it any longer. But you mustn't do anything, Bridie. You really mustn't. I promised Mrs Moffat I wouldn't say a word.'

'Stella,' said Bridie. 'I'm a social worker. Part of my job is caring for children in danger. If you tell me something like this, I can't just pretend I haven't heard. I have personal reasons and I have professional ones, but you must know I'll have to do something. And that's why you told me, and not Heather.'

Stella's colour rose. 'You're not to tell anyone, Bridie, and I mean that.'

'Oh, yes,' said Bridie, making for the door. 'I'm not to tell anyone. Right, Stella. Right.'

She rounded off the last note of sarcasm by wrenching the back door open so hard the ironed pinny shot off its little plastic hook, and fell in starched folds to the floor.

It took Bridie all day to get through to Heather. First she was 'out of the office'. Then she was back, but 'away from her desk now'. Finally, when the secretary said, 'I'm afraid that Miss Palmer's on another line,' Bridie said firmly, 'I'll just hold.'

While she was waiting, she thought about the lunch the week before. All of them had been there. It was supposed to be a surprise party from George for Liddy's birthday – except, of course, that Liddy had to fake it because the sisters had a pact: after the time that Heather was caught with a face pack, no party was ever allowed to be a real surprise; in this they all agreed, and loyalty to one another always outweighed loyalties to boyfriends and lovers and husbands. It was, thought Bridie, one of the reasons they had stayed so close through courting and marriage and, in Liddy's case, sudden, inexplicable divorce. Their father used to tease, apeing in falsetto a song from his own youth about 'devoted sisters'. Eyes raised, they'd bear with him. But all the same, the message had unthinkingly filtered down. The Palmer sisters were close. It was this, as much as their mother's long last years in the wheelchair, that had brought Bridie back from her job in the south, and caused Stella to pick a husband more for his local roots than for his personality. Even ambitious Heather seemed to have chosen assured elevation in the regional office rather than riskier but higher prizes at her firm's London base. From time to time Liddy talked of moving. But only ever to places like Shetland, or Cornwall, or the Hebrides, so none of the others had to take her seriously. In any case, how could she cope without their help as unpaid babysitters and fast response in all emergencies? And, like the rest of them, she'd be quite lost without their constant shopping trips and casual suppers, their loans of books and spare heaters and clothes for special occasions. For years their phones had rung in a ceaseless round of chat about in-laws and job plans and anxieties and triumphs. And there were never any secrets.

Not till now.

She heard a muted click by her ear, and then her sister's voice. 'Stella?'

'No. Bridie.'

'Bridie! How's it going?'

So Bridie had a little moan about the new work appraisals, and the roadworks outside her house. Then Heather brought up the subject of the party, and they chatted about the fact that Liddy had drunk so much champagne that, even on her fourth attempt, she'd failed to blow out all her candles, and had to collapse, giggling, and leave it to George and the children.

'It's Liddy I wanted to talk about, actually. That's why I rang.'

Heather said cheerfully, 'Can't it wait? I'm up to my ears here in paper.'

'What time are you finishing?'

'Not sure. These bank files can take for ever.'

'I could drop in on you on my way home.'

'You'd better have the new code. Punch it in slowly or it doesn't work.'

So Bridie wrote the numbers on her wrist and muttered them through five sets of lights before realizing she was too rattled to learn them. She took the lift to Heather's floor and punched them in under the classy grey sign that said 'Harlow & Courtnay'. Heather came over in a cloud of fresh perfume, and fetched her a mug of coffee from a glistening machine that burbled and hiccuped. Then Bridie told her everything while Heather smoked one cigarette after another.

At the end, Bridie said, 'I thought this office was no smoking.'

'So it is. During work hours.'

'Don't people complain in the morning?'

'I think they blame the cleaners. And I don't work late every night.'

'Just the nights when I want to talk to you.'

Heather didn't smile.

Bridie looked round again. All down one wall were expensively framed certificates with Heather's name. Master of this. Fellow of that. Member of the other. How many qualifications did a person need to manage people's money?

'Nice sofa.'

'The firm's doing very well right now.'

Bridie turned back. 'Oh, come on, Heather!' she cried. 'I'm sitting here waiting. For God's sake, say something.'

'What?'

'Anything. Haven't you been listening? Haven't you anything to say? Can't you at least show a feeling? Express an opinion? Act surprised?'

'Well, that's just it, I suppose,' Heather said guardedly. 'It would just be an act.'

'If you pretended to be surprised?'

Heather nodded.

'Have you suspected all along? Has one of the kids said anything? Has he touched them, or something?'

'Oh, God, Bridie. Touched them! You social workers are the pits! The man's *supposed* to touch them. They're five and eight.'

'Six and nine, actually.'

'Well, anyway!' She wasn't pleased at being corrected. 'He's got every right to touch them. He's practically their bloody stepfather, isn't he? He's been their only real dad for almost a year now. Each time I go, he's cuddling them, and reading them stories, and rubbing Vick on their chests, and generally acting normal.' She paused, deliberately, to watch Bridie's face freeze. 'Yes,' she jeered. '*Normal*. You people have forgotten, stuck in your horrid cheap "interview rooms" with your horrid "dysfunctional families". But out here in the real world, the rest of us are getting by with good old-fashioned *touching*. Everyone feels better for it. You should try stopping being so suspicious.'

Entirely accustomed to tirades about the sick minds of social workers, Bridie found herself homing in on the other thing bothering her. 'So what did you mean before, about not being surprised?'

Heather said irritably, 'It doesn't matter.'

'Yes, it does.'

Heather emptied the ashtray into the waste-paper bin and slid it back in her desk. 'I don't know. I suppose I meant I'm not at all surprised that you're suspicious, given the job you do.'

'That isn't what you meant.'

Heather let out a sharp little laugh. 'Bridie, I think I know what I mean when I open my own mouth to speak!'

Bridie looked out of the window. 'I think you meant that you already knew.'

'No, I didn't.'

Bridie just waited – a professional trick. She certainly didn't expect the sharpest of her sisters to fall for it. But fall for it she did.

'Oh, all right. I did know. I've known for weeks and weeks.'

It fell on Bridie like a stab of pain. She didn't dare look up for fear that the shock of betrayal showed on her face.

'Who told you?'

'Stella, of course.'

'Stella? She told you weeks ago?'

'She told me . . .' Oblivious to the offensiveness of the gesture, Heather flicked back through her diary. 'Way back in June. She was helping me buy a skirt for the partners' summer dinner, and she told me over coffee in Bainbridge's.' She flattened a page, putting a finger on it. 'It was June the third. Saturday.'

'I see.'

Heather started to stuff papers into her briefcase. 'I don't know why you're getting so upset. She said she couldn't stand it any more, and she had to tell somebody.'

'Why didn't you say anything to me?'

Heather said coolly, 'I'm not sure I've had one quiet conversation with you in all that time. There's always the rest of the family about. And I suppose, in our phone calls, it just hasn't happened to come up.'

'Come up? How should something like this just "happen to come up"?'

'*And,*' Heather steamrollered on in her own defence, and Stella's, 'I suppose we were worried about telling you for obvious reasons.'

'And what would those be?'

'Exactly what we're seeing now.'

'Oh, yes? What's that?'

'You know very well what that is. You getting all dramatic,' Heather snapped. 'You thinking something's got to be done straight away. Bridie the social worker getting the bit between her teeth, and knowing instantly what's right for everyone.'

'I'm only thinking about Daisy and Edward.'

'But that's exactly it,' said Heather. 'I might, for example, be thinking more about Liddy.'

Bridie forced herself to stay calm.

'I still don't see why one or the other of you couldn't have mentioned it.'

'*Mentioned* it? It's not just something you *mention*, is it? It's pretty *big*, after all. The man has a court case behind him. Old Mrs Moffat knows someone who knows that George was dragged into court for supposedly putting his fingers up some kid's swimsuit in a public pool. And Daisy and Edward climb on this bloke's knee to have a cuddle twenty times a day. It's not just something you *mention*.'

Bridie couldn't help wondering how she'd ended up in the wrong. She opened her mouth and shut it, till Heather took pity on her. 'Look,' she said, 'I'm sorry, Bridie. I really am. I didn't ask Stella to tell me. She just did. But I can understand why she chose me instead of you. You have to do something about it, and I don't. I can just listen.'

It did make sense, but Bridie was still livid. 'So why do you think she's finally bothered to tell me now?'

Heather shrugged. 'How should I know? I'm not a mind-reader, am I?'

Later that evening, Heather rang Bridie to apologize.

'I'm in the wrong,' she said. 'I should have said something. Or told Stella to tell you.'

23

'That's not really the point,' said Bridie. But it was. All the way home, she'd been seething at both her sisters, close to tears, conjuring up more than one recent conversation. What about the afternoon she'd sat with Heather on Liddy's lawn, watching George toss the children in and out of the paddling pool? One or the other of them must have said, 'He's so good with them, isn't he?' at least a dozen times. Couldn't Heather have said something then? And the walk they took later with Stella over the park to the delicatessen to get bread for supper. 'Liddy's so lucky to find a man who not only cooks, but knows how to make out a shopping list,' she had said. 'A pearl beyond price,' she remembered Heather replying. And fair enough, perhaps, that nothing was said at that moment. But Bridie had gone on to talk about whether Liddy might marry George, if things kept going so well. Surely you'd think that one or the other of them could have said something – anything – even that menacing if incomprehensible little remark of their mother's: 'To see the worm, just pick the apple.' Bridie might not have known what they were getting at. But, looking back, she would at least have had the sense that her sisters were trying, even if ever so slightly, to draw her into the conspiracy they hadn't sought and didn't want. Now, all she was left with was the sickening feeling that they'd been perfectly content to wear their false faces and leave her, the only know-nothing, behind the door.

Well, not the only one, of course. Liddy didn't know either.

'That's not the point,' she said again to Heather. 'But thanks for ringing, anyhow.' Expanding her silent, telly-watching husband into a clutch of impromptu guests filling one another's glasses, she added hastily, 'I can't talk now, though. Dennis and I have people in. I'll ring you tomorrow, shall I?'

Putting the phone down, she went back to watering her plants and thinking about Liddy. Her youngest sister had always been everyone's favourite. There was something about her. It was a sort of coltish, giggling gift for easy living. She could swoop down to seriousness in a moment, if you were in need of it: listen and sympathize, come out with good advice and offers of help and comfort. But the rest of the time she was simply someone to watch with pleasure as she skittered through her days. A husband here, two babies, then a husband gone (and seemingly barely regretted). There was nothing solid about Liddy. Each time you visited, her furniture was moved round, her walls were a different colour, her style had changed. 'Do you want these old curtains? I'm sick of them.' 'Do take that dress. It cost the earth, but if I catch sight of myself in it in one more mirror, I'll go mad.' She was on first-name terms with the bank manager. 'Well, so I ought to be. I practically *live* in his office.' She bought on credit when she had no cash. 'Only four more instalments and all that beastly garden furniture is paid for. Good thing it's gone already, or I'd make a bonfire of it, to celebrate.' 'She'll fetch up in debtors' gaol, that one,' their mother had said, with rising admiration, through the years. (Bridie was of the view she thought a daughter as attractive as Liddy could never get in serious trouble: one flick of her fingers and a dozen moneyed suitors would come running.) And,

'Isn't she *wonderful*?' said everyone else. It was always Liddy who was asked to dip her hand in the tub to pick out the winning ticket, or fire the pistol for the charity race, or swim the first sponsored mile for the photographers.

And no-one was ever jealous. It would have been like being jealous of a child. No wonder nobody wanted to stick a meddling finger in her happiness, and tell her her precious George had a history in faraway Ecclefechan.

But what about Daisy and Edward? Well, what about them? They looked merry enough. They clearly adored George. There were no sideways looks, no dragging back, no always wanting Mum to come along on trips to parks and cinemas. Bridie would put good money on his innocence. She'd bet the roof that, in this case, 'not proven' meant 'not guilty'.

But everyone has a job to do, and this was hers. It couldn't be that after three months of being perfectly content to hear Bridie singing George's praises, and saying not a word, Stella expected her to do nothing.

Bridie put down her watering can and phoned her sister.

'Liddy?'

'Bridie! I was about to ring you! Are you on for this show Heather's got all these seats for on Friday? Have you any idea what time it starts?'

Bridie told her, passing on Heather's warning about the dire parking situation around that particular theatre, and then said casually, 'Speaking of arrangements, can I borrow Daisy for an hour or so this coming Saturday?'

'Borrow Daisy?'

'Just for the afternoon. This friend of mine booked too many seats for something for children, and I as good as promised I'd use up two.'

Before the lie was out, she could hear Liddy bellowing up the stairs. 'Daisy! *Daisy!* Bridie wants to take you to a show on Saturday. Is that all right?'

The rest fell in like clockwork. Edward was howling with outrage within seconds and, through Liddy, Bridie offered him a morning swim. 'Stop *shrieking*, Eddie. Yes, Bridie says there'll be flumes. Shut up! Shut *up!*'

And it was settled. There was a patch more yelling at their end. 'George says do you need an extra lifeguard if he's free?'

'No,' Bridie said. 'I think, this once, it would be nice to be an aunty and do it on my own.'

'Lovely,' said Liddy. 'You're a brick.'

And so she was. She slid down flumes for Edward, and laughed at corny old theatre jokes so Daisy wouldn't feel childish. And cashing in on the wake of both excitements, she led each child in turn up the highways and byways of their little lives, prompting and listening, watching and judging. You could call it unpaid overtime, but, oh, the glorious innocence made it more of a holiday for Bridie. How long had it been since that obliquely raised topic of 'being close' had elicited nothing more suspicious than a small boy's gripe about not being able to see the telly properly when Mum's boyfriend was cuddling him as he read the paper. And it was a long time since Bridie had worked a child Daisy's age gently and imperceptibly round to the subject of secrets, only to hear something as cheerful as a paean of self-praise about a successful surprise party (Well done, Liddy! An Oscar!), and some involuted tale about a lost earring, a wounded frog on cotton wool, and a few quiet suggestions along the lines of, 'Why don't we leave off telling your mum about poor Mr Bounce till she's in a better temper in the morning?'

No, you couldn't fault the man. (Except, perhaps, on putting frogs on cotton wool.) He seemed pretty near perfect. It was a long time since Dennis had bothered trying to protect her from petty horrors that could wait till morning. These days, her own partner seemed rather to relish greeting her at the front door with small domestic *coups de grâce*. 'That bloody washer has packed in again.' 'I should tell you next door's dog has been barking *all day* now.' It would be lovely to live once again with someone who read your every mood, and made your rough places plain, instead of worse.

Bridie pushed open her front door, and eased the shoes off her swollen feet.

'You've been gone long enough,' grumbled Dennis.

'After the show we went to an ice-cream parlour. And then we strolled round the park before I took her home.'

Dennis turned back to the racing. 'My Wife, the Sleuth.'

Bridie could have kicked herself for saying anything the day before. 'Somebody has to act responsibly,' she said. 'And, in the circumstances, don't you think it should have been me?'

She hadn't reckoned with the amount he'd drunk. 'Worst person going,' he announced, not even looking round. 'All you professionals have got sick minds. You go round looking for evil.'

'No, we don't. We simply see so much of it, we learn not to go round in blinkers.'

'So how did it go? Any good clues to break up your sister's marriage?'

'You know they're not married.'

'And you know what I mean. Found yourself any juicy just cause or impediment?'

Bridie disguised her anger so effectively that even she believed herself calm. 'Oh, no. In fact it was very cheering. It's my considered opinion that both of the children love George deeply and sincerely. I'm absolutely certain nothing's going on. Nothing. They seem very balanced and happy.'

'Not like our boys, then.'

Maybe it was his idea of a joke. Or just more rancid backwash from all their recent arguments about Lance storming out to get a flat, and Toby leaving college. Not stopping to ask which, she kicked the kitchen door shut sharply behind her to form a barrier between herself and his needling. Flicking the switch of the electric kettle, she gripped its wide top bar with both her hands and waited, knowing that, if she were lucky and no further provocation floated in from the room behind, its gathering turbulence would, as so often in the past, mercifully and magically absorb her own.

2

IT WAS THEIR SIMPLY LEAVING IT THAT SO AMAZED HER. Weren't there a thousand excuses in a family for picking up the phone? 'You know that old video of ours that keeps sticking? Well, I was all for tossing it out, but then it occurred to me that one of your lads might want to tinker with it. And, by the way, Bridie, have you had time to have a think about that business we were talking about?'

But nothing. Silence. All the calls Heather made were carefully timed to hit the answerphone. 'Oh, bugger. I suppose you're at Tesco's. Never mind. I'll try again.' And Stella, of course, managed to steer the content of her weekly on-the-dot clock-in down all the usual blind alleys: the weather, Neil's medication, the noise from the overpass that was constantly making them think about moving. And then, just as Bridie might have pounced, – 'Stella, about what you were saying . . .' – she'd be off. 'Oh, God, Bridie. I've just remembered I was supposed to pick up some stuff for Neil twenty minutes ago. I'll have to go.'

What were the two of them thinking – that it wasn't all that important? Admittedly neither of them spent the hours Bridie did, unravelling the miseries of family betrayal and trying to arrange for children sucked into squalid, guilty half-lives to grow again towards the light. But they weren't daft either, surely. They read the papers. They must know that things like this shouldn't be ignored. It wasn't just the normal run of gossip. At root, it didn't matter if Mr Faithless slept with Mrs Fun, and those who suspected said nothing. The safety of children is a different matter. Why didn't either of them *ask*?

She put the question to Dennis in his more chastened moments, but he refused to see what was bothering her. 'What on earth does it matter?' he kept saying. 'So long as you're confident everything's all right. Maybe your sisters think the less said, the better. Presumably they passed the problem on to you because it's up your alley. I expect they just reckon that, if you can let it drop, then so can they.'

'Maybe,' said Bridie. But she couldn't help wondering what it was about people who presumably thought themselves sentient and caring that made them so easily able to assume that all the right wheels were turning. Her files at work were peppered with optimistic utterances. 'Mrs F. said she rang twice, so she thought someone must be dealing with the matter.' 'When he didn't hear anything back from the council, Mr S. reckoned everything must be all right.'

Those same files bulged with the results.

'I just don't understand why neither of them has even bothered to ask what I've done about it.'

'Perhaps they're embarrassed.'

'Embarrassed!' But he was probably right. On this topic, as on so many others, Dennis was the man on the Clapham omnibus, and once again Bridie had to force herself to remember that everyone looks at the world through the prism of their own life. It was important to keep a sense of proportion, and not let the cancer of contempt nibble away at her feelings for both of her sisters.

'Should I raise it myself, do you think? Or let it lie?'

Dennis heaved about uncomfortably on the sofa where he spent far too much of his time now. 'How can I tell you what to do?'

True. And, back in the office, this sort of thing wouldn't hold her up for a moment. She'd slide into the usual procedures without a moment's thought. Agree a Plan, Set a Date and Make a Note.

'I'll wait, I think. Give them a month and see if either of them brings it up again.'

'Fair enough. That sounds sensible.'

And so it did. So why did Bridie feel uncomfortable, as if she were quite cold-bloodedly giving her sisters time enough, like lengths of rope, to hang themselves in her esteem?

'Maybe it'll come up on Sunday,' she tried to absolve herself.

'What's happening on Sunday?'

'It's on the calendar. We're all going to Stella's.'

'Oh,' Dennis groaned. 'The Summer *Stint*.'

Bridie and Liddy lay side by side on Stella's perfect lawn.

'You stay on that stripe,' said Liddy. 'And I'll stay on this one.'

'Ssh!' Bridie reproved her. 'Neil will hear you.'

'He knows what I think,' said Liddy. She raised her voice across the garden. 'Don't you, Neil? You know what I reckon about you and your lawn.'

Neil raised his glass to her, and turned to tell Dennis in the other deckchair, 'She reckons I need psychiatric help.'

'Don't we all?' Dennis said. 'Being related to this lot.'

'When I prise myself out of this nice lounger,' Heather said, 'no-one is to snaffle it. Is that understood?'

Dennis looked at her hopefully. 'If you're going into the house, could you fetch me another beer?'

'It might be a good idea to bring out that jug of juice,' Stella said, just a little too brightly.

'Are there any more of those little squashy things with sour cream on the top?' asked Liddy. She lifted her head suddenly. 'Where are the children?'

'George took them off,' said Heather.

'Where?'

'To the shop. For ice lollies.'

'In the car?'

'No. Walking.'

'Walking!' Liddy was ecstatic. 'That's twenty minutes, isn't it, Stella? There and back.'

'At least,' agreed Stella.

Liddy lay back again and stretched. 'The man's a *gem*,' she announced proudly. 'A perfect *gem*.'

Bridie held her breath, waiting and watching. Heather prised herself out of the lounger, pretending that she hadn't heard, and Stella busily started to brush stray strands of cress through the little fretwork holes in the metal garden table.

'Don't do that,' Neil told her. 'You'll make the grass look terrible.'

'See,' Heather said, gathering up Dennis's beer cans. 'Liddy's quite right, Neil. You need psychiatric help about your lawn.'

And so the moment passed. Bridie tried catching Heather's eye as she walked past. Was it wise, she wanted to ask her with a look, to help the issue slide away so easily? But Heather busily looked somewhere else. Down it came with the usual force, the great wall of sisterly censure; but this time it wasn't Bridie's disapproval of them, but theirs of her. She could guess what Heather was thinking. Here is the sister who lectures us on what to think, and how to vote, and even who we ought to feel sorry for. And yet she can't see that she's making a mountain out of this molehill. Here is a decent man, doing his best by Liddy, and Bridie wants to wash her conscience clean at everyone's expense, trying to raise an issue that will poison everything, and make everyone unhappy – *everyone* – just to 'do the right thing'. And that can't be the right thing, can it?

And as for Stella, she was probably just wishing the whole business well away. After all, hadn't she spent the whole of yesterday cleaning the house, and trekking round Sainsbury's, and making those special squashy things with sour cream on the top, and God knows what else, so everyone could have a perfect day? Even the sun had made an effort to come out, and stay out. It wasn't often that the whole family came round to her. (Their house was so much further out than everyone else's, and not all the family cared too much for Neil.) So why, when everything had come together beautifully, should Bridie get a chance to spoil things? Good thing that Heather had so skilfully steered everyone away from trouble.

Bridie considered going after Heather to catch her alone in the kitchen. But she'd made her decision to give them time, and, in any event, Liddy was off again.

'He's wonderful.' She was speaking more softly now, so only Bridie could hear. 'Especially in bed. He treats me like a princess. And he's not just wonderful. He's different. Every single time.'

'Different?'

'You know. One night he'll spring out of the bathroom with some old flower clenched between his teeth, and throw himself at my feet. The next night he'll slide between the sheets and take over totally.' Liddy managed to make her imitation sound quite menacing. ' "Please don't struggle. I don't want to have to hurt you." I find myself almost worrying about jackboots ruining the sheets.' Her eyes were shining. 'Then, the next time, he'll go all French on me.'

'Disgusting!' Bridie said obligingly.

It was a moment before Liddy got the joke. And then she shrieked.

'You're the one who's disgusting, Bridie!'

'Is Bridie letting down the side again?' Neil called over. 'Here's me and Stella trying to have a nice family afternoon with nothing to scandalize the neighbours, and Bridie sets out to ruin it!'

Maybe he just said it. Maybe. There was, thought Bridie, no reason on earth for her to think that he'd been primed, and what he'd said had a double meaning. But it occurred to her all the same. And that was the problem when you started with secrets. As she tried to explain to Dennis on the drive home, once a family moved off the bedrock of openness, it was hard to believe remarks like that were just the same old jokes as usual, made in good faith. Secrecy poisons everything.

Dennis thought she was mad. 'You're drunk,' he said. 'Or the sun's gone to your head. It's quite ridiculous to think old Neil was showing you the yellow card. I didn't even hear him say it.'

'Just because you didn't hear it—'

'Oh, shut up, Bridie, for God's sake!' Clearly the beer had made him snappy. 'It was a nice afternoon. Everyone got on well. Heather never once mentioned investments. Neil didn't go on and on about his bloody lawnmower service contract. The kids weren't forever splashing water and hurling balls about—'

'They were hardly there!'

'Just what I mean. And for once you didn't keep sending Liddy off into floods with all your gruesome case studies. Even Stella sat on her bum for minutes on end, and didn't scuttle round pouncing on my beer cans and

Heather's cigarette ends. All in all it was a lovely after-noon. So why go spoiling it now?'

'I'm not *spoiling* it,' said Bridie. 'I'm trying to *discuss* it.'

'Well, not with me, you can't,' said Dennis, 'because I had too good a time.'

'Yes,' Bridie said, 'about four cans too good, if you ask me.'

'I didn't, though, did I?'

They sat in silence till they reached the ring road, when Dennis apologized and Bridie, sensing a problem with the clutch, prudently forgave him.

A couple of weeks later, Bridie came home to find Heather's car in the driveway, blocking the garage, and Heather on the sofa grooming the dog with a hairbrush she'd taken from the shelf in the downstairs cloakroom.

'You're very late.'

'Meeting,' explained Bridie. 'That's my best hairbrush you're using.'

'He's *matted*, Bridie. You ought to be ashamed.' She pulled the old dog closer to get at the rest of him. 'Shouldn't she, Harry boy?'

'He hates being groomed.'

'Not with this brush.'

Bridie sighed. 'Where's Dennis?'

'He rang. Not back till later. Something to do with Toby.'

'Lance,' Bridie corrected, remembering. 'He's moving flats again, and needed a little bit of help with the van hire.'

'Oh, right.' But Heather, having no children of her own, took no interest in the boring bits about other people's. 'I'm here', she said, 'to ask what you've done about this stupid George business.'

'What makes you think I've done anything?'

'Come off it, Bridie. We all know you. You must have come to some decision. What was all that about taking Daisy and Edward out? Don't try to tell me your head wasn't full of wee motors, because I don't believe it.'

Bridie's relief was immediate. Back came that comfortable, safe feeling that there were some things sisters couldn't hide. How could uncertainty gnaw at you, guilt poison your days, when the sister whose toy you'd broken, pet you'd lost, or dress you'd stained could tell at a glance that you were the villain and claim instant restitution with a slap, a vicious tug of your hair, or a wail down the stairs at your mother? In families, order is restored with such stern swiftness there's no time for insecurity. No time to brood. And it was practically impossible to drift from the bedrock of your proper self. Only a single child could make the horrible mistake of trying to get through her days in some unsuitable and ill-fitting disguise. With a sister, there'd always be someone there to snatch it straight off again.

'I'll make some tea.'

But Heather pointed to the tumbler she'd moved round the edge of the sofa, away from Harry's thumping tail. 'Sorry. I'm afraid I've already cracked and pinched some of your whisky.'

How cheering, thought Bridie. How very cheering and nice to come home to someone so close and easy that she can scrabble under your flowerpots to find your key, and start in on your dog, and fix herself a drink, and get straight to her point in an instant. When she came home to Dennis now, the atmosphere was little short of dispiriting. They'd pick their way through all the statutory questions about his job applications and her day's work, judging one another's moods, decoding the answers. Bridie would find herself lifting the lid of the kitchen bin to gauge the number of discarded beer cans while Dennis strained his ears from the living room to hear her do it. And all there was to look forward to was the endless drab negotiation their marriage had become. 'I'll peel the potatoes if you fix that plug on the toaster.' 'I'm putting the stuff in the washer, so can you feed Harry, please?' 'If I put the car away, will you do the dishes?' As if both of them felt each day of their togetherness already chewed up enough of their lives for it not to be fair to have to do, as extra sacrifice, extra waste, more than their absolute fair share of evening chores.

Instead, tonight, here was cool, professional Heather, with her shoes kicked off and her arms around Harry.

'You ought to get a dog of your own, you know.'

'Oh, Bridie, don't be daft. I'm never home.'

'It's such a shame. You can see how much he adores you. He never rolls over like that for me.'

Heather started on Harry's fat rump with the hairbrush. 'So go on. Tell me everything.'

Bridie explained about the hours she'd spent with Daisy and Edward.

'You can tell, then? Just get them chatting and pick up the clues?'

'Usually. Especially with children you know well.'

'And you're quite confident?'

'As confident as I can be. Put it this way, if this was work, I'd definitely close the file.'

'Good.'

Heather put down the brush and fished for her tumbler round behind the sofa. Then she leaned back, and Harry forlornly accepted his transition from object of devoted attention to mere footrest.

'So that's it, then?' asked Heather. 'Can I tell Stella everything's all right?'

'Do. I'm rather surprised she hasn't spoken to me herself.'

'You know she's frightened of you.'

'Of course she isn't.'

'Yes, she is. I expect it's all your opinions, and odd lines on everything.'

'I don't have odd lines on everything. I just try to think things through a bit.'

'And Stella just gets on with things.'

They both knew the things that Stella just got on with: finding the perfect swag rail; seeking out the right lavatory-brush holder to match her new bathroom suite; crimping her pastry edges; keeping her freezer filled with recipes from magazines her sisters never even noticed in shops, let alone thought of having delivered. She was a mystery. Looking back, it appeared as if Stella had floated through childhood with neither passions nor interests.

She'd simply grown, not calling attention to herself in any way. No-one would ever have burst through a door saying, 'Guess what Stella's done now!' or, 'Have you heard Stella's plan?' or, 'Stella thinks . . .' With all the others around, nobody even noticed. But then she'd bumped into Neil, and, overnight, it seemed, the Stella-in-waiting bloomed. Nothing was said. But suddenly the house was filled with Stella's ring, and Stella's wedding list, and Stella's dress and veil. Finally, thank God, Neil took her off (past Stella's pew plan, through Stella's Order of Service and into Stella's reception). The two of them disappeared into Stella's new house, and there they both carried on: Stella and Neil's plan for the garden, Stella's rotisserie oven, Neil's new hedge clippers. It was indeed a marriage of true minds.

'You'll tell her, then, that everything's all right?'

'And we'll forget the whole business.'

'Right.' Bridie wondered whether to add the tricky little rider now. Better not, maybe. But it was not in her nature to lay low and hope that things wouldn't come up. 'Unless, of course . . .'

'Unless what?'

'Unless they decide to get married.'

'Oh, God!' Heather made a face.

'Don't look like that. The thought must have occurred to you.'

'I suppose so.'

'You do agree that it would change the situation?'

Heather peered in her drink. 'I don't see what difference it makes really, him practically living there the way he does, and the two of them getting married.'

'I think it does a bit.'

'Not to the children, since you're so sure that things are fine.'

'No, not to them. But to Liddy. How would you like to find out, after your wedding, that all your guests knew something that you didn't know about your own new husband? I think I'd hate it.'

'Do as you would be done by, are you saying?'

'I think so.'

'Oh really!' Heather paddled her toes in irritation till even besotted Harry staggered to his feet and moved away. 'What's the big difference between *acting* married and *getting* married?'

'I don't know,' Bridie wailed. 'I just know that there is one. There's something *special* about getting married. That's why people do it, for heaven's sake.' She reached down for the hairbrush Heather had abandoned, and started picking out the fluff. 'I mean, if she found out now that we knew this stupid rumour, I could stick up for myself and say I thought it really was for the best not to say anything. But if she were about to make promises – take serious vows – it would be different. I'd think, at that point, she really should have been told.'

'And you think she might think that too?'

'Wouldn't you?'

Heather shrugged. 'So that's the deal, then, is it? First sign of wedding bells and we tell Liddy?'

'I think so.'

'Right.' It was decided. 'Next time I see Stella, I'll tell her.' Heather finished her drink just as Dennis came in and

tried to talk her into having another. To Bridie's astonishment, he showed the keenest interest in what had
brought his sister-in-law round to their house, and even
after Heather had gone, and Bridie and he were undres-
sing, she caught him still muttering about it. 'No, it *can't*
have been Heather . . .'

Bridie poked her head back round the bathroom door
and said through a mouthful of froth, '*What* can't have
been Heather?'

He looked up, startled. 'I was just thinking that it can't
have been Heather who wanted to know what you'd
decided to do.'

'Why not?'

'Heather? Come off it!' He shoved a leg in his pyjama
trousers. 'When did Heather ever give a damn about
anything? No, it must have been Stella.'

She made a little froth-bound questioning noise. But he
didn't notice. He was nodding away to himself confidently. 'Out of the pair of them? Oh, I should think so.
Stella. Definitely Stella . . .'

3

IT WAS NOT UNTIL DECEMBER THAT LIDDY ANNOUNCED SHE was going to get married.

'Not a big wedding,' she said. 'Nothing like yours, Stella. Just the family, and George's parents and brother, a few friends, and, of course, Daisy and Edward.'

Heather was the first to recover. 'That's brilliant!' she said. 'Congratulations, Liddy!'

Bridie dived for the loophole her sister had offered her. 'You mustn't say "Congratulations" to Liddy! That's very rude. You're supposed to congratulate the man, not the woman.'

George stepped forward and waited. There was no retreat.

'Congratulations!' said Heather.

'Congratulations!' said Stella.

Bridie saw no way out. 'Congratulations, George!' she said, and rushed over to Liddy's corner cupboard. 'What have you got in here, Liddy, that's suitable for the occasion?'

'It has to be champagne,' said Stella. 'Neil and I will nip out and fetch some.'

'No,' Bridie insisted. 'You two have only just got here. Heather and I will go.'

Dennis, of course, screwed up her one chance of getting a quiet word with her sister by saying, 'No, I'll go, Bridie.' Since it was his usual role, nobody argued, and while he was gone, Stella kept the pot bubbling nicely with talk of the wording of invitations to second marriages and the relative merits of linen wedding suits and ivory silk dresses. '*March*, though,' she kept worrying. 'It's so *un-dependable*. You never *know*.'

'It won't matter,' said Liddy. She was in her enchanted child mode. She kept laying her hand on George's arm as if she couldn't quite believe him real, and beaming at everyone, and rebuking herself for not having her fridge already brimful of champagne. 'We weren't going to rush into anything, you see. But then one morning I woke up and the bedroom was filled with the most glorious pink and silver light, and I thought to myself, Why are we *waiting*?'

'But you've settled on March, though,' Bridie said, curious.

'That's when George's brother gets back from his job in Singapore. And it's after the anniversaries.'

The anniversaries were 29th February (an awkward date for their father to have died because it meant that they could only think of him on the right day one year out of four), and 4th March for their mother.

Stella, the only sister to lean towards sentiment, was torn. 'You could leave it till April, Liddy.'

'No,' Liddy said. She squeezed George's arm again. 'Now we've decided, I can hardly wait. It's March. The last weekend in March.'

Bridie looked round for the children. Edward was on his knees in the corner, fitting the tiniest wheels she'd ever seen back on a toy police car. And Daisy was on the sofa with the headphones on, supposedly watching television, but, since her thumb stayed on the buttons of the remote control, Bridie suspected she was listening. Had the news come as a surprise? Bridie thought back to Daisy's chatter in the ice-cream parlour, and realized how little of what her niece had said about George had stuck in her mind. Like one of those nice people you meet at parties twice a year and come to dread because the welcoming smiles and friendly openings never lead on to anything, there was a cheerful opacity about the man. With anyone else, she might have put it down to a child's inability to find the right words. But he'd not made a dent on any of them, really. Neil was a great one for adopting people, for golf, or villa holidays, or one of his organized charity quiz teams; and yet he didn't seem to have made very much headway with George. She wouldn't have expected Dennis to make an effort. (Efforts of any sort seemed more and more beyond his powers.) And as for Heather and Stella, they'd been content, as she had, to let George's growing bond with their sister form the only real tie. He'd slid into the family without a fuss. But there's the world of difference to a child between 'Mum's boyfriend' and 'my stepfather'.

For all her apparent excitement, Liddy didn't fail to notice that Bridie's eyes had come to rest on Daisy. 'The children are thrilled,' she said very firmly. 'Absolutely delighted. Both of them.'

Bridie recognized a raised storm cone when she saw it. Liddy was clearly going to be in no mood for lectures from off-duty social workers about not rushing decisions that would be important to her whole family, just because of a bit of pink and silver light. 'Dennis should be back at any moment,' she said. 'I'll find the glasses.' She fled into Liddy's kitchen, where every surface was piled high with stuff for lunch. 'Who brought these smoked salmon things?' she called out. 'Are they yours, Stella? Are we allowed to nibble them with the champagne?'

'They were supposed to be the starters,' fretted Stella. But then the momentousness of the occasion swept even her along. 'Oh, go on, then. Cut them up smaller and set them out on one of those . . .' But Bridie's food-presentation skills were notorious. 'No. Leave it. I'll do it.' She dived into the kitchen after Bridie, who took the opportunity to brush the door closed behind her as if by accident, and turn to look meaningfully at her sister.

'Well!' Bridie said.

But Stella was having none of it. Instantly she walked past Bridie for the pepper mill she didn't need, and pushed the door open again.

Meekly, Bridie allowed Stella to prise the knife she'd chosen from her grip, and give her another with which to make a better job of cutting the smoked salmon things into neat, bite-sized pieces. Through the open door, she could hear George going on about how wonderful Liddy was, and Liddy fizzing with ideas for places to go on a honeymoon with children. She longed for Dennis to get back, not just because now she was desperate for a drink, but also because the more of them in the house who were in on the problem, the better. She'd feel less of a traitor to her starry-eyed sister if everyone in the silent conspiracy, the conspiracy not to be silent any longer, was gathered under the roof feeling just as uneasy, just as much of a louse.

And guilty, too. They should have seen this coming. *Did* see it coming, in fact. But now that it was here, their weeks of hopeful discretion just made the whole thing worse. It had been wrong and idiotic of them not to tell Liddy at once. And it was going to make things so much more unpleasant telling her now, a full six months after Mrs Moffat first opened her mouth. A full five months since Heather first heard the news in Bainbridge's. A full four months since she herself took Daisy and Edward out, preferring to nose around in their little lives, rather than speak openly to their mother. They were in trouble, every one of them. They'd gambled, and they'd got it wrong.

But the day of the storm is never the day for thatching. (One of their mother's less inscrutable utterances.) Bridie was still ruefully reflecting on the significance of timing in family matters when Dennis kicked open the back door and staggered in.

'Not a crate! Not a whole crate!'

'Oh, come on, Bridie. It was an excellent deal. We can use quite a bit of it ourselves over Christmas. And a wedding is a wedding.'

Not to seem churlish, Bridie didn't point out that the announcement of future plans was scarcely a wedding.

And Stella was still clucking round. 'These glasses are horribly pitted, Liddy. You're not still using that dishwasher stuff I warned you about, are you?' It was hardly the moment to hint that, after their own little surprise announcement (if it was a surprise), this ceremony might not ever come off. So she prudently took the car keys off Dennis, and let him get on with what he was good at — popping corks and having a good time. She raised her glass dutifully each time anyone said anything nice about Liddy or George or the coming celebration. And no-one could have faulted her as a supportive sister, or known that, while she was gritting her teeth through all Neil's laborious toasts to George's new 'Second-hand Rose' and Daisy and Edward's prospective 'Wicked Stepfather', she was back into work mode, setting objectives, deciding on timing, and making little mental notes.

'So what's her name going to be, then?'

'She'll keep her own name, surely.'

'Well, probably. But what's his? I've forgotten.'

'I'm not sure.' Bridie did a brain-search. 'It's Rigsby, isn't it?'

'*Rigsby?*' Heather cackled down the phone. 'Lydia Rigsby!'

After a spasm of merriment, they went back to the subject in hand. Telling Liddy.

'We could at least play down the fact that we've known for months. Wouldn't it seem a whole lot more casual if we left her with the impression that Mrs Moffat has only just mentioned it?'

'Suggest the poor woman just happened to drop the bombshell in her Christmas card?'

'Christmas card?' Bridie was floored.

'Bridie, Mrs Moffat went back to Ecclefechan in September.'

'What, for *good*?'

'Apparently.'

Bridie was astonished. 'How come Stella never even mentioned it?'

'She has to me. For weeks now, all I've been hearing from her is the perils and horrors of finding a new cleaning lady.'

'She never said a word to me.'

The silence at the end of the line confirmed Bridie's sinking feeling that this came as no surprise to Heather. And when she thought about it, she'd known for months – no, if she were honest, for *years* – that the content of her conversations with Stella could not possibly reflect Stella's real life. (For one thing, she'd have to be brain dead.) It was presumably in self-defence – because, as Heather claimed, Stella was frightened of Bridie – that Stella had, a number of years ago, corralled a few safe old telephonic ponies, to be let out at the same time each week, and trotted round for twenty minutes or so. 'All we ever seem to talk about is my boys and her shopping.'

'That's good, then,' teased Heather. 'This'll be something new.'

Bridie's heart sank. 'Can't we just leave her out of this?'

'Of course we can't leave her out of it. Don't you think Liddy's going to be on the phone to Stella within seconds to find out exactly what Mrs Moffat said? She's got to be warned, or she'll kill us.' There was a pause. 'But we could just speak to George. Tell him what we've heard, and say, as Liddy's sisters, we feel we must be sure that she's been told. Ask if he's done that, and, if he hasn't, suggest he gets on with it.'

'I've been thinking about that, but it won't quite do.'

'Why not?'

'Because he might not tell her properly. He might just mutter something about spiteful rumours – not enough to let her make a proper informed decision about something to do with her own life, but just enough so, if we ever bring it up, she's likely to cut us off with, "Oh, I've heard all about that, thanks."'

'I suppose so.' Heather sighed. 'And there's that business of it not being fair.'

'Fair?'

'Of course, if he really is a sleazeball, then that wouldn't matter. He'd just deserve it. But Stella did point out that, if anyone says anything directly to George, they will have let the poor man know that, on the verge of his new life, all three of his sisters-in-law know the seedy whispers about him.'

'I hadn't thought of that. What a grim start! And we do think he's innocent, don't we?'

'Well, I do,' said Heather. 'And you sounded even more sure than I am. And Stella—'

'Oh, Stella!' Bridie sighed. 'Sometimes I think she's too morally vapid to think ill of anyone she likes, or who likes her.'

'Tut, tut!'

'Well,' Bridie defended herself sourly. 'It's *true.*'

'God, you're judgemental.'

'I can't help it. It comes with the job. You either end up judging nobody, or judging everyone.'

'I'm glad I'm not one of your victims.'

'Clients,' said Bridie, for the millionth time.

Back on familiar ground, the conversation ended easily. 'Well,' Bridie said. 'Who's going to warn Stella that the balloon's going up?'

'She's not going to like it, you know. When I left Liddy's, she was knee-deep in chat about bouquets and canapés. To her, we'll be party poopers. She's going to want to drop the whole damn thing.'

'I thought you cleared all this with her. "The first faint tinkle of wedding bells, and we tell Liddy."'

'She as good as agreed. But now it comes to it . . .'

'Who's going to speak to her, then? Shall I?'

'You? You have to be joking, Bridie! Leave this to me.'

Heather rang back the next day.

'So,' Bridie asked. 'How did it go?'

'It was like talking to treacle,' Heather complained. 'You could sort of keep pushing her one way, but then she kept sort of seeping back. She kept saying, "But Liddy's so *happy*. I don't want to be part of spoiling that."'

'Did you point out that if a little bit of gossip can spoil Liddy's happiness, it can't be worth all that much?'

'No, Bridie,' Heather said tartly. 'Nor did I bother to point out the further corollary that if being told this does spoil everything for Liddy, then that proves it was definitely the right decision to tell her.'

'Quite right,' said Bridie. 'Best not to dabble in cor-ollaries.' She paused to check the word had come out right, then, when Heather didn't correct her, she went on. 'So, tell me. You pushed and pushed, but did you get anywhere?'

'God knows. As far as I can make out, all Stella's worried about is the two of us putting an end to all her cosy chats with Liddy about matching sandwich fillings and wedding-bell napkins. I'll tell you Stella's trouble. She and Neil have run out of places to put things. This is the first chance she's had in years to shop and shop and not have to shove the results in her own bloody cupboards.'

'I could sneak round and burn down their house. That would get her back shopping for herself pretty sharpish.'

There was neither a chuckle nor an answer. Heather was brooding silently down the line.

'So what happens now?' Bridie asked finally.

'We could leave it . . .'

'Because it didn't come out first time round?'

'*You* try, then,' Heather snapped. 'You're trained to deal with people with no brains and even less moral sense. *You* have a go.'

So Bridie had a go. First she tried inventing a credible excuse to visit Stella.

'I could pretend I'd just dropped in because I was passing.'

'Oh, yes,' scoffed Dennis. 'Twelve years she's lived there. We've lived here eight. And, suddenly, you're passing.'

'All right, then. I could go round to ask her advice on something.'

Dennis laughed.

'I could *deliver* something. What a pity they're all coming here on Christmas Eve. It'll look odd if I take round their presents. Can you think of anything else?'

'I do remember her saying that round her way you could never find rubber kitchen gloves in medium in the blue. Why don't you take her round a pair of those?'

Bridie eyed him suspiciously before hurling the dish-cloth. 'Dennis!'

He reached out for her hopefully, but she brushed him away. So he went off. She heard the faint *phut* as he prised up the tab on his beer can. 'I'll tell you, Bridie,' he called back. 'Don't waste your time. You're on a hiding to nothing. You could show up on their doorstep at midnight, torn, raped and bleeding. But the minute you mentioned Liddy's wedding, Stella would know you'd staged it. So give up.'

So she gave up, and just went round. She found Stella in the middle of 'getting straight before Christmas', which appeared to mean furiously rinsing her dustbins. At her most conciliatory, Bridie said nothing, and wiped her feet carefully as Stella led her into the house. She sat at one end of the sofa next to a perfect little spinney of bonsai and waited for the subject of the wedding to come up naturally.

Stella, however, was on guard. She led off with the usual questions about Toby and Lance, then worked her way through the weather to the increase in noise from the overpass on cold, still days. That took her on to Neil's headaches. And once she'd reached Neil's medication, it seemed she was holed up nicely, ready for a siege, though perfectly happy to put out the occasional feeler to see if Bridie would prefer to talk about their mother. 'Do you remember how she couldn't look at a medicine bottle without saying, "Each doctor just makes work for the next"?'

'Stella,' said Bridie, defeated. 'About this wedding—'

Stella picked a leaf too small to see off one of the bonsai. 'Is that what you've come round to talk about?'

It was astonishing, thought Bridie, how guilty her sister's question made her feel. 'I'm worried about Liddy.'

The moment the words were out of her mouth she regretted them. Stella had only just hinted that this visit of hers was an aberration. Now Bridie had as good as admitted that, but for Liddy, she wouldn't have come round at all. Was Stella hurt, she wondered? They'd all assumed she was too wrapped up in her house and her shopping to notice that, though she and Neil were always invited to family celebrations, and there was a high turnout for their own, there were a raft of other contacts between the sisters from which she was often excluded. This 'dropping in' business, for example. All of them traded on the fact that Stella's house was too far out, and not on the way to anywhere. But it was possible Stella felt left out and offended. She certainly wasn't making things easy now.

Bridie got to the point. 'The thing is, Stella, we just wanted to check you're still with us on making sure Liddy knows about this weird rumour before she goes on with her wedding plans.'

Stella was silent. Bridie had the impression she was looking for more blighted leaves on her bonsai.

'Heather came round to talk to you about it, but—'

'But?'

The tone wasn't welcoming.

'But she came away not sure you were convinced.'

'Well, she was right. Because I'm not.'

Bridie tried 'active listening', a technique she'd been taught in her very early training. 'You think maybe we should all just forget the whole business.'

'Yes,' Stella said. 'Yes, I do.'

'You think it's not likely he did anything, so there's no point in ruffling Liddy's feathers.'

'That's right.'

'And Heather and I are being over-scrupulous.'

'Bridie,' snapped Stella. 'Stop telling me what I think. I *know* what I think already. The problem's not that I don't know what I think. It's that Heather and you don't *agree* with me.'

Bridie abandoned active listening. 'Listen, Stella,' she said irritably. 'You are one hundred per cent in the wrong about all this. We've been Liddy's sisters all our lives. Staying close to her is important. Now along comes this bloke. I grant he's wonderful and he makes her happy. But he's only been in the picture for a couple of years, and just because he goes to bed with her, that doesn't mean he's automatically so important that our relationship with her no longer matters. Because it *does*. How are you going to feel, facing Liddy in the future, knowing that you know something she doesn't? Won't that make you uneasy?'

'I don't see why,' said Stella. 'It hasn't yet.' But she sounded uneasy already.

'You don't feel a sliver of dishonesty about keeping quiet?'

'No, I don't. I just think it's sensible.'

'Really?' persisted Bridie. 'Even when she goes on and on about how wonderful George is with Daisy and Edward? You don't feel there's this little thing she really should have been told? A little nugget of silence that makes you uncomfortable?'

Stella sprang to her feet, and started shifting porcelain nuns along the mantelpiece. 'Listen, Bridie. I'm not like you. I don't have to dig into things all the time. I'm content to let people get on with their own lives, and be happy.'

'But Liddy won't be that happy if she finds out that we've been keeping from her something about her own husband.'

Stella turned from the mirror. Her eyes were marble hard, and her voice, when she finally spoke, was little short of icy. 'I think I'm happy to risk it.'

Bridie put the coffee mug she'd been nursing back in the bonsai spinney.

'She's your *sister*,' she pleaded. 'Don't you at least think we should be straight with her? Because I feel that very strongly, and so does Heather.'

There was an element of warning in Stella's reply. 'I doubt if Heather feels it as strongly as you do, Bridie.'

'You know she does. She came round here to tell you. She agrees with me.'

Stella said huffily, 'I don't know why you've both bothered to come round here, then. Since you're so *sure*.'

Resenting her tone, Bridie said rather meanly, 'I suppose we've both bothered to come round because this whole business really began with you.' And then she felt

58

guilty because, though she'd managed to pick different words, the childhood accusation, 'You started it!' still rang in her ears, and Stella was clearly rattled.

'I wish I'd never even mentioned it!'

Bridie leaped at the opportunity to make amends. 'But that's exactly why you did,' she said earnestly. 'Because these things fester when they're left as horrid little secrets. And if you don't tell someone about things in their own life that might make a difference to the decisions they make, it's really the same as lying.'

'Oh, that's ridiculous!'

'No, it isn't,' Bridie insisted. 'What's there to choose between telling lies and acting the clam? They both leave people not knowing where they are.' In the hope Stella would buckle under her barrage, Bridie pressed on. 'Suppose some bloke's having an affair. His wife finds out, and says, "How could you deceive me?" And he says, "I never deceived you. It's just that you never asked, so I never said anything." Is he a liar, or isn't he? What's the difference?'

For a while, Stella had no reply. Finally she responded, 'You might be good at arguments, Bridie. But that doesn't mean you're always right.'

'I know,' said Bridie. 'And, believe me, the last thing I'm bothered about right now is winning some stupid argument. What I care about most is keeping a very precious sister.'

At this, astonishingly, Stella capitulated. 'All right,' she said, as if dismissing every last reservation. 'Go ahead. Do it your way. Maybe it's for the best.'

Bridie was mystified as to how she'd suddenly managed to press the right button. It was only an hour later, pulling into her own street, that it struck her that Stella might have misunderstood, and thought perhaps she was the precious sister Bridie had in mind.

Bridie felt terrible. But there was nothing to be done. It was hardly the sort of thing you could go back and explain. And, after all, permission is permission.

Again, Dennis was interested. 'So Our Lady of Colour-Coordination gave you the go-ahead, did she?'

'I think I persuaded her,' said Bridie. 'But, then again, with Stella you can never tell. It's possible that all I did was bully her into submission.'

'You'd know best about that!'

Bridie pretended that she hadn't heard. 'That's the trouble with weak people,' she said, as she unlaced her boots. 'You bat on at them till they crack, and you end up convincing yourself that you've made a convert. But all you've ever really made is an enemy.'

Dennis stopped in his tracks on his way to the kitchen. 'Sometimes you astonish me, Bridie. You really do.' But Bridie was still too hurt from his last gibe to ask him why. Instead, she simply said as coldly as possible, 'All part of the service,' and put her boots underneath the chair, where she'd be able to find them without trouble in the morning.

4

'WE'LL TOSS,' SAID HEATHER.

They'd just been through the whole thing, firstly agreeing the phone was the only way (a visit would seem too personal, too significant), and also deciding to make the call together, so there'd be two of them to vouch for exactly how little was said, and how casually they'd said it, in case anyone should accuse them of exaggerating later.

And, to this end, they'd settled on Heather's office.

'On your speaker phone? Do you mean we'll be having a three-way chat?'

'That's a *conference* phone.'

'All we have here is phones.'

'Stop playing Bridie in Underfunded Land,' said Heather, 'and look at your diary. How about tonight?'

'Tonight?' For a moment Bridie assumed that Heather had finally been seized, like herself, with the urgency of the situation. But, no.

'If it's not tonight, then it can't be for days. I'm not doing this in work hours, with everyone listening. And tomorrow it's badminton. Wednesday, I have other plans. Thursday's always difficult because—'

'Tonight, then,' said Bridie, who had a deskful of her own in front of her. 'Just tell me who's going to do it.'

And that's when Heather laughed.

'We'll toss.'

Bridie didn't reach Harlow & Courtnay till seven o'clock, but people were still leaving.

'You lot must work even harder than we do.'

'I expect we make fewer mistakes, too.'

Bridie turned to the closet for a hanger. Usually, she took jokes about her profession in good part, but now, after spending a whole day thinking about which of the two of them should make the call, she was feeling a good deal more sensitive. 'Your mistakes matter a whole lot less, of course,' she said, dismissing Heather and money and Harlow & Courtnay in one fell blow.

Heather made peace. 'I'm dreading this, Bridie. It's been on my mind all day. Do you want coffee before the execution? I'd offer you something stronger, but this is an alcohol-free office.'

'Really?' Bridie was interested. 'You have a policy? We just have a vague sense of self-preservation.'

'Start, and you'd never stop?' Heather cleared one of the guest chairs for her sister. 'Make yourself comfortable.'

Bridie felt sick with panic. You couldn't, she thought, have chosen a worse sister to be on the receiving end of this call than poor old Liddy. The rest of them were probably capable of taking news like this in their stride, having proved themselves over the years fairly adept at turning the odd blind eye, and not querying some pretty questionable explanations. But not Liddy. Oh, not Liddy. She had a positive fetish for the truth. She was a ferret for 'what Sam really meant', or 'what Max's behaviour really proved'. To her, people were soulmates, or nothing. She went on courses aimed at developing her 'inner self', presumably so she'd be more alive to even greater intimacy with those in her charmed circle. To Liddy, 'feeling close' was some sort of psychic equivalent to simultaneous orgasm (and pursued, as a mystic ideal, quite as assiduously as others pursued the latter). Even when Liddy was young, no boy was ever allowed to lie to her. Caught out just once, and that was it: he got the final flick, and any excuse along the lines of 'I didn't think you'd want to know' was a total non-starter. The other sisters were different. Stella, in Bridie's view, took very good care never to be told anything that might ruffle her feathers. Heather was so indifferent to matters of feeling and the heart that she would as often as not simply forget the things her lovers had summoned their courage to confess to her. And Bridie had always been able to distract herself with questions about why the person concerned should have felt the need to lie in the first place. But Liddy! Liddy would gaze into her new lover's eyes (after she'd learned his star sign and decided on the nature and colour of his aura) and he was supposed to have bared the whole of his background and history before Liddy even considered baring anything of her own even halfway as intimate.

Pray God this bit of gossip wasn't news.

'Ready?' said Heather, and reached for the speaker phone. Clearly the notion of tossing for the honour had gone straight out of the window, Bridie couldn't help noticing. And probably just as well. If she herself made the call, it would be freighted with all her professional baggage, and look as if she'd been chosen because of her experience in 'difficult matters'. It might even appear to Liddy as if, instead of casually passing on some silly piece of gossip, her sisters attributed to it some significance and importance. Better let Heather do it. She was, in any case, punching out the numbers with astonishing speed.

'This'll be like the dentist, I promise you. Over before you know it.'

It was, too.

'You're making this up.' Liddy's voice echoed, small and tinny, but incredulous, round the lush office in which her sisters eyed one another with unease. 'You're making all this up.'

'I know it must sound like it.' (Rather disquietingly, Heather appeared to Bridie to be saying this into the air, not even looking at the telephone, let alone holding any sort of receiver.) 'It's so *ridiculous*. It's just that we thought, in case George hadn't bothered to mention it, you ought to know. So if someone ever comes up to you at a party or something, and—'

'It's not true. It's rubbish. It's a pack of vicious lies.'

'I'm sure it is,' soothed Heather. 'I'm sure it's all absolute nonsense. A horrible mistake.'

'No!' Liddy's voice shot up so high it set the speaker box reverberating, till Heather reached out to damp it with a touch. 'I mean *you're* lying. You're just a pack of jealous bitches making all this up, and I don't believe a word of it.'

At that moment, watching her sister open her mouth to speak, Bridie knew for a fact that telephoning was a big mistake.

'*Ask* him, Liddy,' Heather said testily. 'It's perfectly simple. Just *ask* him.'

Both of them flinched horribly at the sound of Liddy's phone slamming down on its cradle. 'Well,' Heather said, lighting a fresh cigarette from the one already smouldering in the ashtray. 'I handled that really well, didn't I?'

'Never mind,' Bridie said, adding, though she wasn't at all sure she believed it, 'It probably wouldn't have gone any better if I'd been the one to do it.'

'Still,' Heather said, 'I shouldn't have got ratty. It's just that I don't take to being insulted.'

'Few people do.'

Heather pushed back her chair and went over to the window. 'She's got a bloody cheek, calling me a liar.'

'And me and Stella. We're all in on this. Don't take it personally. She called us all liars.'

'And bitches! Jealous bitches. Did you hear that?' Heather was getting worked up now.

'Yes,' Bridie said. 'I was listening.'

'I wonder what she's going to do now.'

For answer, the phone rang.

Heather dived for the speaker, but even though Bridie didn't know which button to protect, she got her hand there first. 'Calm down,' she warned. 'Stay cool. No point in getting in a spat just because you're offended.'

'Quite right,' said Heather. Astonishingly, she cooled down at once. Taking one last drag from her cigarette, she pushed the button and said, more calmly than Bridie could believe, 'Liddy! I'm glad you rang back. I was just about to—'

Dennis's voice cut in.

'Heather? Is that you? What's going on? Have you got Bridie with you?'

'Dennis!' said Heather. 'Yes. She's here.'

'I've just had Liddy on the phone,' said Dennis. 'She's in a bloody state, I must say. What on earth have the two of you done to her?'

With a gesture, Heather offered the speaker phone to Bridie, but Bridie shook her head.

'We haven't done anything,' said Heather. 'Except tell her.'

'Well, you'd better warn Bridie to watch her rear mirror when she's driving home. Because I've just had an earful of obscenities, and I wouldn't like to pass on what Liddy phoned up to call Bridie.'

'A bitch?' suggested Heather. 'A vicious, jealous, lying bitch?'

'That's about it,' said Dennis. 'Well, it's good to know you two shit-stirrers are keeping your fingers on the pulse.' And he hung up.

'Charming!' said Heather. 'Is he always that support-ive?' But Bridie was well past caring about Dennis. She was reaching for Heather's cigarettes. 'I hope these aren't menthol,' she said, taking one and holding it inexpertly between her fingers. 'I hate menthol cigarettes. They parch my throat for days.'

'That's right,' said Heather, lighting it for her. 'When in deep doodoo, think only about something stupid. I expect it's a habit you've picked up from your poor unfortunates.'

'Clients,' said Bridie, but her heart wasn't in it.

Then the phone rang again. It was Liddy.

'Is Bridie there with you?' she asked, without preamble. 'Is she there – *earwigging*?'

The sheer hostility in her voice made Heather panic. 'No. No-one's here. This isn't that big a deal, Liddy. Honestly, it was only a matter of keeping you up to date with something we all knew, but weren't sure you did.'

Liddy's tone was icy. 'Heather, I'm not a halfwit. I *know* she's there. And I know what she's up to. You can tell her that from me.' They waited expectantly, but, two miles away, the phone went down again with another bang, and they were left staring at one another across the desk.

'That was quite menacing,' admitted Heather.

'Why *me*?' Bridie asked, rattled. 'Why pick on *me*?'

Heather leaned back thoughtfully. 'That's right. I was the one who made the call, after all. Isn't that curious?'

'You don't seem very bothered,' Bridie said testily.

'Bothered?'

'Upset. You're taking all this a bit clinically, aren't you?'

'Don't start on me,' snapped Heather. 'I'm doing my bit. I've done what you asked me.'

'*Asked* you?' Bridie was furious. 'We *agreed*.'

'We didn't just *agree*, Bridie. You know that. We agreed with *you*. You were the one pushing this all along. Everyone else was for leaving it.'

'But you *agreed*.'

'All right! All right! I *agreed*. But don't push your luck. Don't expect me to get my knickers in a twist just because Liddy didn't like what she heard. Leave her. She'll calm down in her own good time.'

With *you*, thought Bridie with sudden prescience. With you, perhaps. But not so quickly with me.

'Bridie?' Heather leaned forward. 'Bridie, are you *crying*?'

Angrily, Bridie brushed the tears away. 'No, I'm not crying. I'm just *upset*. It's been a horrible day. It's been horrible thinking about it. And it's been horrible doing it. And I hate the fact that Liddy doesn't understand, and just thinks we're . . .' She couldn't say 'jealous bitches', so her voice trailed away.

'She'll get over it,' said Heather. 'She's just upset. She's furious with him for not telling her – because it's obvious, isn't it, that he hasn't told her. Not one word. And she's furious with us for knowing. When she's calmed down and had a little weep, and hurled a few dishes at him, and made up in bed, and he's promised never to keep anything from her again, she'll be all right. Before we know where we are, she'll be ringing us up and acting as if it never happened. Honestly, she will.'

'I hope you're right,' said Bridie. But what she said bore no relation at all to what she thought. For, deep inside, Bridie knew Liddy had put the black cap on her head when she said, 'I know what she's up to.' Those words were a staple for Bridie. She'd heard them in a thousand interviews. She knew what they presaged. She recognized the oceanic rumblings of hate. Through Bridie's office had trailed a line years long of bitter ex-husbands, slighted mothers-in-law and resentful stepchildren, all saying, 'I know what she's up to' in exactly those tones. In all that time, had Bridie ever once managed to persuade someone – truly, sincerely, and not just to pass some social worker's test – that 'she' wasn't up to anything really; she was just doing what she thought was best?

No. Never, probably. Not ever. No.

By the time she got home, Bridie had moved from her weepy stage into one of cold indifference. Let Liddy bloody get on with it. If she couldn't see that no-one had any vested interest in spoiling things for her and George, that was her problem. Only somebody quite determined to play the martyr could truly believe her sisters were out to spread gossip from simple spite. In fact, Bridie thought uncharitably, the three of them had quite a lot to gain from Liddy settling down and marrying George, and living happily ever after. George, after all, had a reasonably good job. (Heather had had to 'lend' Liddy money several times since the death of their mother.) There would be two adults in the house. (Bridie and Dennis had taken Daisy and Edward dozens of times when Liddy was on weekend courses, or weak from flu.) And Stella – well, Stella, being more out of things, had less to gain from George's proving permanent. But, even so, she would have had nothing in mind but the welfare of her sister. So if Liddy was going to be ungenerous enough to think the worst, then good luck to her. Bridie could simply not be bothered. She clattered round the kitchen, scouring the rings round the burners on her gas stove, scraping charred cheese off the grill pan, attacking the grease film over the oven door. This must be what Stella did most days. And how Heather felt most of the time – minus the anger, of course, because Heather was famous for 'not really caring'. Arrangements would be made, and suddenly it would turn out that there had been some mix-up with the dates, and Heather couldn't come. 'Shall we change it to another day?' someone would offer. And Heather would just shrug. 'I'm not that bothered. I'll see you all soon enough. So don't worry.'

And no-one did because, at heart, they knew that it was true. She wasn't bothered. (Stella, on the other hand, could have gone round saying, 'I don't mind, honestly,' till she went blue, but nobody would have believed her.)

No. Heather was a cool one. Keeping her distance, she only fell in love with married men, and love was not the proper word for those strange, etiolated partnerships that lasted over years – their very stability, thought Bridie, stemming from just that unmagic mix of mutual indifference and convenience that made Heather's affairs like other people's marriages, and often made them last as long.

What a sense of freedom was in this! Her oven sparkling, Bridie moved on to an energetic wiping of all her other kitchen appliances. What did it matter, anyway? Who else would be that bothered if one of their sisters got in such a pet? No-one she knew. At work, the closeness of Bridie's family was matter for remark, sometimes in tones of admiration or envy, but, just as often, in terms of gentle derision. 'Out with the family mafia again, Bridie?' 'The same old gang, is it, this weekend?' And yet it wasn't as if the crying need for one another's support was still a part of their lives. No, that was gone now. Dead, and safely buried. Gripping the back of a chair, Bridie leaned over the palely gleaming kitchen table as the old faintness swept through her and the voice in her ear sounded as strong and real as if not just the years had peeled away, but half her skin as well.

'Who left Daddy's best handsaw out in the rain and ruined it?'

Dennis had been astonished when they first mentioned it. 'Your father called this a *game*?'

'He enjoyed it.'

'So did we,' Liddy had reminded Bridie. 'If he did it at all, it meant he was in a good mood.'

'Let me get this straight. He went round the dinner table and, one by one, made you all cry?'

'Stella was always first. She was a pushover. You only had to say to her, "Who trod on Daddy's freshly varnished floor?" and she'd be flooding. Tears in her potatoes. Gravy quite thinned out.'

'Then me,' claimed Liddy. 'I was always next. "Who let the boys next door see her bare bottom?" Off I'd go.' At Dennis's look of utter disbelief, she added hastily, 'Not when I was older, of course. He had to try a little harder then.'

'Christ,' Dennis muttered. He'd turned to Bridie. 'And you were the ruined handsaw. So what about Heather?'

'Oh, Heather was a hard nugget. Heather was difficult. Sometimes she nearly didn't crack.'

'That's right,' said Liddy. 'Sometimes you'd look at Heather across the table, and you'd think, She's going to make it this time.'

'She never did, though.'

'Once,' Liddy defended their other, absent sister.

'Not really,' Bridie said sternly. 'She cried her eyes out afterwards.'

'But he didn't know that.'

'Of course he knew. Mother would have told him.'

Dennis was still shuddering. 'Horrible, horrible! And once you were all in tears, what happened then?'

'Oh, you know,' said Bridie. '"Can't any of you take a little joke?" About what you'd expect from a man.'

'Not this man,' he'd told her so fiercely she couldn't help but believe him. And when, later that evening, he'd talked of love, and altering his plans so they could stay together, she'd felt a whole new safety net spread out beneath her. It hadn't interfered with earlier loyalties, though. The Palmer sisters had stayed close. Too close, perhaps. Dennis had even hinted at it once or twice in earlier years when he'd tried suggesting they invite a

72

colleague here, an old school friend there. 'Well,' Bridie would say, always ostensibly willing, but puzzling over her diary. 'This weekend's out, of course, because of Daisy's christening, and the party afterwards. I don't think we'll feel like having people the next day. And the Saturday after we're supposed to go boating, and then back to Stella's . . .' She'd riffle through more pages. 'The weekend after that's fine,' she'd admit dubiously. But naturally Dennis couldn't bring himself to say casually to another man, 'Why don't you and your wife pop over for supper – nothing special, mind – in three weeks' time?' It had to be this weekend, or nothing. So it was nothing, of course – except that, by the time the empty weekend rolled round, it would be filled with pizzas at Liddy's, or tea on Stella's lawn, or using up a couple of Heather's leftover freebie client tickets. The comforting, nurturing, family gang.

And on these occasions, everyone was smiles and hugs. But did they, like Bridie, give the family any real thought in between sightings? Liddy, of course, was far too dizzy for sustained reflection. Stella, absorbed in her piles of magazines and catalogues, would probably not have had the time. But what about Heather? Did she, like Bridie, go home and think, Liddy looked peaky today. I wonder if she's worrying about something, or, Stella was obviously hurt that she was phoned last about those tickets? No, it was more likely, thought Bridie, that Heather did what, from way back, they all recalled her doing: shut her door on the whole lot of them, switched on her music, and lay, starfish fashion, on the floor, filling her mind with the anguish of dead composers and the intricacies of their skills, rather than, like Bridie, minting her own worries freshly by the day, and sifting the complexities that seemed to surround her.

'Oh, fine for some!' Bridie muttered, slamming her cloth in the bucket, and pressing a cloud of grey out into pristine water. 'Fine for some! It's very easy, if you decide you're not prepared to get involved!'

But was it? Not for Bridie, obviously. As Dennis rather meanly pointed out, she wasn't doing very well.

'At what?'

'Not getting involved. Didn't you march in here a couple of hours ago saying you'd had enough, you were only doing your best, and, for all you cared, Liddy could think what she sodding well liked? Now you're crouched over that bucket grumbling like an old witch, quite as upset as when you walked in here.'

'At least the kitchen's clean,' Bridie said sourly.

Though it was small comfort that it was.

5

IT CAME IN USEFUL, THOUGH, WHEN, FOUR DAYS LATER, Stella ran out of excuses and had to admit she could probably drop by on her way back from shopping for Christmas in Adnitt's.

'Oh, look! You've got a new oven!'

Bridie explained. And all the chat about the wonders of all-purpose cleaners bridged the embarrassment nicely, putting Stella at her ease till Bridie could bring herself to raise the topic of the day.

'About this Liddy business . . .'

Stella became nervous all over again. 'I do think she's very upset,' she offered warily.

For tactical advantage, Bridie pretended to misunderstand. 'I'm not at all surprised. It must be horrible for her to find that someone as close as George hasn't been straight with her.'

'No,' Stella said even more carefully. 'I think she's upset with you and Heather.'

'Because of our phone call?'

'Yes.'

'So you have spoken to her?'

Stella paused. Was she, thought Bridie, wondering if she could get away with barefaced lies? But no. With a marked lack of ease, the answer came. 'Of course I've spoken to her.'

'There's no "of course" about it,' Bridie said. 'She's not answering any of *my* calls.'

Stella looked politely concerned.

'So what did she say?' Bridie pursued the matter.

Stella inspected her fingers. 'I think she thinks it was mean and unnecessary to pass on nasty gossip about George.'

Bridie stamped on her rising irritation. It was the sheer mealy-mouthedness of all these 'I think she feels . . .' and 'I think she thinks . . .' that got to her most.

'But when you *explained* to her . . . ?'

'Explained?'

'About us all agreeing it was the only thing to do.'

Stella looked doubtful. 'I don't think I ever agreed it was the only thing, Bridie.'

'Well, then. The *best* thing. The *right* thing.'

'I don't think I'm sure of that, either.'

'Maybe you're not, in retrospect,' said Bridie. 'But at the time you did agree. So what did Liddy say when you told her that?'

Stella went back to her fingers.

'Stella,' said Bridie. 'You have told Liddy you were in on this?'

'She didn't really want to talk about it, you know. I think she's too upset.'

'But it's *important*,' said Bridie. 'You have to talk about it with her. Otherwise she might not realize you were part of it. She might carry on thinking it was just me and Heather trying to cause trouble. You have to make it clear to her that you agreed it was the right thing to do.'

'I'm not sure it was, though. Liddy's so upset.'

'But that's not the point! The point is that Liddy's blaming us as if we're *enemies*. She doesn't like what she's heard, so she's shooting the messenger. But you can still get through to her. You can explain.'

Stella's face was unreadable.

'Look,' Bridie said. 'We need your support here. If you go sympathizing too much because she's upset, she'll settle down to believing she's dumped her anger in the right place – on me and Heather. She won't bother to look a bit harder and see why she's really mad.'

'I don't think there's very much I can do.'

'You can do plenty. For one thing, you can stick up for me and Heather.'

'I am sticking up for you.'

'How?'

Stella shook herself irritably. 'I can't explain, Bridie. I just *am*.'

Bridie was suddenly deeply suspicious. 'So what did she say when you pointed out that we all agreed she should be told?'

'I don't think we quite got round to that.'

Bridie's frustration boiled into rage. 'What do you *mean*, you didn't quite get round to it? You *spoke* to her, didn't you? What's there to *say*, except, "Look, Liddy. It's not fair getting mad at Bridie and Heather if you're not getting mad at me, too, because, on this one, we're like that!"?' Bridie's clamped fingers came so close to Stella's face that she recoiled.

'Stop getting at me, Bridie!'

'Getting at you? I'm not *getting* at you. I'm trying to find out what you said to Liddy.'

'I've told you what I said.'

'No, you haven't.'

'I tried to stick up for you. Really, I did.'

'*How?*'

'I told her you didn't mean it.'

'Didn't mean it?' Bridie was mystified. 'What do you mean, you told her we didn't mean it?'

'I said you were probably sorry.'

'Sorry? For telling her something that she had to know?'

'She didn't have to know, Bridie. I told you that from the start. In fact, I *kept* telling you.'

It was a good thing Dennis walked through the door and sensed the coming blast. Not even stopping to take off his coat, he seized his sister-in-law by the arm. 'Stella!' he said. 'The very woman! Now come outside and tell me if last night's frost has done for my pelargoniums, or if it's worth trying to save them.'

Stella was off her chair and out of the room in a moment. Dennis turned hastily to Bridie. 'You'd better get upstairs, quick. Before you explode.'

And Bridie fled. Coming towards her in the mirror on the landing, she saw a face she barely recognized, twisted with anger and contempt. She lay flat on her back on the bed, hating Stella. Parts of her seemed to be not even touching the counterpane, she was so stiff with rage. Was Stella absolutely *stupid*? How could a person with sufficient brains to walk in a straight line apparently prove so incapable of taking on board the damage she was doing? Each ounce of sympathy she fed to Liddy lessened the chances of their sister understanding why they'd done what they'd done. It was hard to believe that Stella couldn't see that what she was doing was the very worst thing – for Liddy, for Daisy and Edward (after all, fuelled with the notion of her sisters' spite, why should Liddy now bother to look at George with more appraising eyes?), and certainly for Heather and herself. Outside the window, she could hear Dennis determinedly chuntering on about the merits of geraniums as Stella edged prudently towards her car. And as its door slammed shut and the engine fired, Bridie tried once again to force her muscles to unknot.

But how could Stella do it? How could she rat on them like that? If she'd been so sure that telling Liddy was the wrong thing to do, she should have argued harder. She should have made her position clear. 'I'm having none of this,' she should have said, and then given her reasons and tried to persuade them. But now, because of her spineless habit of caving in always to the last one to speak, she'd dropped them right in it, made a difficult situation impossible, and as good as betrayed them. She had betrayed them utterly.

'I *hate* her,' she said to Dennis when he came in. 'I absolutely *hate* her. Liddy at least has the excuse of not thinking straight because she's so upset. Stella has no excuse at all.'

Dennis plonked himself down in the old nursing chair in the corner, and said nothing.

'She's so *stupid*,' said Bridie. 'Stupid and craven, that's what she is. I could *strangle* her. Honestly! My own bloody sister!'

Dennis stretched out his legs, and put the beer can he'd brought up with him beside the small forest of framed photographs of Bridie's family on the dresser at his elbow.

'I could *murder* her,' said Bridie. 'What does she think she's doing? Does she think at all? Can't she see what she'll make Liddy think?'

Dennis turned the nearest family photo to face the wall.

'I just hope Liddy comes to her senses,' said Bridie. 'How long can it take someone who's known you forty years to realize that, if you've never been mean before, you're probably not being mean now?'

Dennis twisted the photo back a quarter turn.

'And George might help,' said Bridie. 'He might not have had the guts to tell her himself, but surely he'll see why we felt we had to, and stick up for us. He always seemed a reasonable enough bloke.'

Dennis twisted the photo back a little further. Bridie shot up on the bed. 'This is *ridiculous*,' she said. 'I don't know why I'm worrying. How can a family as close as ours fall apart because of something as stupid as this?'

Dennis turned the photo right round to face the front again.

'It's a storm in a teacup,' said Bridie. 'Heather's quite right. My problem is, I'm rushing things. Liddy needs time to calm down and come to her senses. And Stella probably believes she's doing the right thing, pouring oil on troubled waters.'

She swung her legs round off the bed. 'That's it,' she said. 'I'm not going to let it get to me. Liddy's got to calm down, after all, because she's due here on Christmas Eve. She can't back out of that. She has to come to the party.'

Was the word 'party' a trigger? Dennis lifted the tab on his beer can, and Bridie looked at him properly for the first time.

'How many's that?'

Dennis glanced down.

'Actually,' he said, not even bothering to disguise his astonishment, 'I think it's my first.'

'I can see why you're cross with her,' said Heather.

'Cross? I'm not cross. I'm *incandescent*,' said Bridie. But she couldn't help looking and sounding cheerful enough, because the lunch had been lovely and, as if by agreement, they'd managed to stay off the topic right the way through to the coffee. Beyond the faintly steamed windows, the bright December afternoon turned magically from pink to blue. Beside her knees, Bridie's bags rustled to remind her of a successful morning's shopping. And Heather had been kind, pressing her to the expensive end of the menu, and making it clear that she'd be picking up the bill.

'I'll tell you what annoys me most,' Bridie went on. 'The way she keeps saying she's trying. "I'm doing my best," she says. But she certainly seems to be making quite sure that her best doesn't ruffle Liddy's feathers. I tell her practically every day, "You've got to be firmer with her. Make it clear you're with us on this one, and she's got to think it through." And all I get is, "Well, Liddy thinks . . ." and "Liddy feels . . ." and "Liddy's very upset, you know." It doesn't even seem to occur to her that Liddy's feelings don't count for everything in the world.'

'Got to leave some room for yours?'

Bridie stared, taken aback, not just by her sister's needling remark, but also by the rush of dislike she suddenly felt for her. Cold-hearted and complacent cow! Just because she took so little to heart herself, there was no reason to be so scathing with other people. But Bridie found a safer way of batting back. She found herself saying loftily, 'I suppose someone in my profession comes across all too many people who've let their "feelings" take precedence over doing the right thing. And they do tend to act rather despicably as a consequence.'

'Well, preaching at Stella won't help.' The unspoken 'nor at me' hung over the table as Heather delved in her bag for her purse, then picked out a credit card and laid it on the table. 'It just makes her think we haven't understood how strongly Liddy feels about all this.'

'How much of a huff she's in, you mean.'

Heather just shrugged, catching the waiter's eye as he walked out of the kitchen. He came over at once.

'I can't help it,' said Bridie. 'I tell Stella how upsetting all this is for us, and all she comes up with is stuff like, "Well, maybe it's right for Liddy to stay away from you two right now." '

'Well, maybe it is.'

'How can it be? Things aren't just "right for someone at some time". They're right or wrong. They're either right for everyone all the time, or not at all. And all this indulging Liddy isn't going to help when we have to be civil at my party.'

'Liddy's not coming to your party. Didn't you know?'

It was a horrid blow. Bridie was grateful to the waiter for coming back then with the credit slip, and hovering over them, offering a pen, and dutifully tipping the last of the mineral water into the glasses as Heather added on the service. 'There,' she said, pushing everything towards him. The waiter ripped out his bits and disappeared. But still Bridie couldn't speak. Heather was looking at her curiously.

'You really didn't know.'

'How should I know,' snapped Bridie, 'if nobody's bothered to tell me?'

'Be reasonable,' said Heather. 'How can she come to your party if she's not talking to you?'

Bridie sat in cold shock. She'd held a party every Christmas Eve since she'd left home. Stella skipped three years in a row, off on the 'seasonal breaks' that she and Neil spent so much of the rest of the year discussing. The winter their mother was dying, the party was a wash-out. And on one or two occasions Liddy had had tonsillitis, and had collapsed into Bridie's bed before anything even got started. But no-one had ever simply 'not come'.

Heather was gathering her things. Hadn't she even realized what she'd said? Bridie was desperate to delay her. 'But what about Daisy and Edward?'

Embarrassed, Heather shrugged. 'I really ought to be getting back. I have a ton of stuff to shift before I go home.'

Bridie lowered her head to hide the bright wash in her eyes. 'I'll say goodbye to you here, shall I?' She forced her voice to stay steady. 'I want to repack some of this shopping in the Ladies'.'

Heather took her seat again. 'Look,' she said. 'I realize what I said was a shock. It wouldn't have come out like that, but I thought you realized.'

'How would I realize?'

'Well, it's obvious. If people aren't even speaking . . .'

'She's not talking to you either, but you can handle it. You're still planning on coming?' She glanced up. 'Aren't you?'

'Of course I'm coming.'

But Bridie hadn't missed the little flicker of unease. 'She *isn't* talking to you, is she?'

'Not really, no.'

'What do you mean, "not really"? Either she is, or she isn't. Is she, or isn't she?'

'Don't hector me, Bridie.'

Bridie's voice rose, disturbing the people at neighbouring tables. 'I just want to *know*, that's all!'

'We've spoken once or twice, that's all. And pretty briefly. Nothing was said. Just what she said to Stella, that she's upset, and she thinks it was mean of us to pass on gossip about George.' To stop Bridie pushing for details, she scraped back her chair and stood up again. 'I've so much to do, honestly. I really do have to go. I'll phone you tomorrow about food for the party.' On her way between the tables, she bent to kiss Bridie's cheek. 'Stop worrying. It'll sort itself out. There's still a whole week, remember. Maybe she'll come to her senses. Be a brave little soldier.'

Since this was one of their mother's ludicrous little blandishments, it only made things worse. Bridie struggled with tears all the way down the stairs to the Ladies'. No wonder the lack of contact between herself and Heather had lasted the whole week. Bridie had thought it odd that, since they parted at the car park that evening, with Heather saying so confidently, 'Just leave her. She'll calm down,' there hadn't been a single call along the lines of, 'Heard from Liddy yet?' or, 'Any word from Our Lady of Disenchantment?' She'd put it down to Heather's sheer indifference. She had assumed that, irked with the whole tiresome business, Heather had simply gone home and shut the door. And that was why Bridie hadn't rung her first – to give her the space she so obviously needed. Indeed, part of the pleasure of this invitation to lunch had come from presuming that there was a message hidden away in it: 'I'm fed up with everyone else, but not with you.'

But, no. It turned out that the spur was guilt. More a case of, 'I'm back talking to Liddy now, so I'd better make sure I stay straight with you.' But how had Heather managed to break through Liddy's great wall of silence? Was Liddy not ignoring her calls, the way she'd ignored all of Bridie's? Or had Heather *written* without telling her? If so, what had she said? Bridie sat on the wobbling lavatory seat feeling miserable, confused, and unspeakably lonely. Around her, her plastic bags sagged. The end of the paper roll was disgustingly crumpled, and now her party was ruined. Bridie wept, furious with Liddy for thinking ill of her, with Stella for perfidy, and with Heather for her sheer uncommunicative insensitivity.

A worried voice came over the partition. 'Are you all right in there?'

Oh, God! Oh, God! 'I'm fine, thanks. Honestly.' Hastily, Bridie pulled up her pants and tights.

'Are you sure? Can I fetch someone? Can I get you a taxi?'

For heaven's sake! The world was crawling with foul, inconsiderate people and Bridie had to end up in the adjoining cubicle to Mary Poppins's mother. 'No, honestly. Really. I'm just a tiny bit upset. My cat died yesterday. I'll be over it in a moment. You're very kind, though. Thank you.'

Go *away*.

The running sympathy ebbed along with the timed tap flow. 'Well, if you're *sure* . . .'

'I'm sure. Honestly. Thank you. Goodbye.'

Bridie sat, howling inside, for just a little longer. Then she stood up and got a grip, first of her shopping, and then of her flailing emotions. She did the best she could with her tear-streaked, lugubrious face in the mirror, and spoiled herself rotten with a taxi home.

Dennis, unfortunately, was standing by the window. 'Good lunch, then?' he said, with a look at the taxi still doing a nine-point turn because of the Pickford's van blocking the Easter Road exit.

'Horrid!' said Bridie, dumping her shopping. 'Horrid!'

'Didn't you go to the usual place?'

'It wasn't that.' And out it poured. He didn't seem too shocked. So Bridie followed him into the kitchen and explained again.

'I got it the first time,' said Dennis.

'You don't seem very bothered.'

Dennis could furnish neither a convincing argument nor a convincing look to prove he was.

'You don't give a shit, do you?'

Dennis turned, pointing a teaspoon. 'Don't growl at me', he warned, 'because all your meddling has made you fall out with your precious sisters.'

'I wasn't *meddling*.'

'Liddy obviously thinks you were.'

'But she's not *thinking*, is she? She's just *upset*.'

Her snappy tone silenced Dennis, but did nothing to damp down her own anxieties. Liddy had to be thinking *something*, or she'd have been just as upset with Stella and Heather. So Bridie stamped round the house a bit, and then came back to ask Dennis, 'All right, then. Tell me why I've been picked out for Principal Sinner.'

'Because you're Chief Bossy-Boots,' suggested Dennis.

'Oh, thanks very much! That's most helpful!'

'It could be that.' Dennis defended his theory. 'After all, when was any Palmer ever allowed to do anything without you stirring the pot first? Even your poor old mother wasn't allowed to die till you'd dragged Heather back from Bermuda.'

Tears spurted out of Bridie's eyes. 'But I thought – I thought . . .'

Instantly, Dennis softened. 'Of *course* you did, Bridie. And all your grisly little psychology books are probably right. In the long run, it probably is best for people to' – even through her distress she could hear the distaste in his voice – '"say goodbye properly". But your mother was dead two days later. So what the hell? And, as for Heather . . .'

He didn't have to say it. Both of them knew that, left to herself, Heather would have preferred to finish her very expensive holiday undisturbed, and come home to perform in some pious but undemanding sororial duet. 'If only I'd *known*.' 'We did try and get in touch with you, Heather.' 'Well, never mind.'

'I get everything wrong,' said Bridie. Her tears were flowing now. 'Are you saying we shouldn't have told Liddy, either?'

'I don't know,' Dennis said. 'I don't understand your family. I don't understand why everything has to *matter* all the time. Why you have to have all these *feelings*. I don't see why, once you're grown up, people have to stay special because they're *family*. What have you got in common with Stella? Nothing. In fact, the rest of you spend your whole time secretly scoffing at her and Neil. And Heather's as selfish as sin. The only one who was ever a good laugh was Liddy.' The words he couldn't bring himself to say rang round the room. 'And now she's gone.'

Bridie used the flat of her hands to wipe the tears off her cheeks. Dennis was right again. Everyone fretted too much (except for Heather). She'd go back to letting them all get on with it. Not care. Not mind. Not give a damn.

So it was surprising that she brought it up quite so quickly at the last team support group before they all knocked off for Christmas. Terence asked, 'Any problems?' as usual. And Bridie half listened through the usual work difficulties. One of Sarah's clients was frightening her. She couldn't put a finger on it exactly, what it was, but she still somehow felt a little threatened. Miss Minto's voice trembled as she spoke about the pitiful holiday arrangements for the only child saved from the Turner Street flat fire. And Len was worried that he so disliked the husband in one of his families that he might have been unreasonable about the man's Christmas access. Everyone had barely finished putting in their twopenn'orth about that, when Bridie found herself saying, 'Suppose . . .'

They all fell about laughing. ('Suppose' was their communal code for a personal problem.) Bridie went back through how it all began, and then adeptly cut the story off on the day of the phone call to Liddy. 'So should we tell her?'

'Of course you should,' Terence said firmly. 'I can't think how you're doubting it.'

No-one demurred.

'How do you think she'll take it?'

There was more disagreement here. 'She'll be upset,' said Sarah. 'That's only natural. But not with you, I shouldn't think.'

'If everyone dumped their foul moods on the people who deserved them,' Terence reminded her, 'we'd all be out of a job.'

'But this is Bridie's *sister*.'

'Close families are the worst,' observed Miss Minto. 'When they fall out, there's no-one around to distract them. They just seem to fester and brood.'

'That's nice for poor Bridie!' said Terence. But Bridie comforted the embarrassed Miss Minto by saying, 'No, honestly. I think Ruth's right.' Into her mind had sprung another of her mother's strange mutterings, 'Pet lamb, cross ram.' She'd never understood it. Or, rather, she'd assumed it meant only what was quite obvious: that a spoiled child would turn into a bad-tempered adult. But now she saw there was another layer to it. If everything went well, and life was smooth, anyone could be merry and generous. It didn't prove a thing. The only real test of what sort of person you were came when you had to work against the grain to do the right thing. Bewitched, love-struck Liddy was not prepared to face even a shade of disappointment about her intimacy with George. It was easier to shoot the messenger. And Bridie was surprised. But why? Where was the evidence for this great assumption that, put in a hard place, Liddy would make an effort? If someone couldn't save to buy their garden furniture, or stint themselves a little to pay their bills, why should the people around them assume they'd have the strength of character to lay the blame for a tarnished dream where it belonged?

Terence was speaking to her. 'Never mind, Bridie. Even if your sister does shoot her stack, you've got two others to stand up for you.'

As Bridie knew from her failures, it is as easy to fool a social worker as anyone else. She lifted a cleared face.

'That's true,' she said brightly. 'I'd forgotten that.'

6

THE PARTY WAS GHASTLY – WORSE THAN A FUNERAL TEA. AT
least if they'd just buried Liddy, they would have been
able to say her name. It would have been natural to talk
about times when she'd been around, or mutual friends. As
it was, everyone had to steer away from any topic that
might bring her to mind. Some were better at this than
others. Heather stuck to investments, and Neil's lawnmower service contract had a good long, if unseasonal,
conversational run. But everything raised by Stella seemed
to run into some sort of verbal emergency braking lane,
with everyone hearing the unspoken 'but Liddy says', or,
'and Liddy thinks', as clearly as if she hadn't had the
foresight to snap off in mid-sentence, pretending to choke
on a forkful of lasagne, or a limp piece of lettuce.

And that was another problem. The food was dire.
There's all the difference in the world between cooking in
happy anticipation and cooking in dread, and Bridie's sour
spirits had affected everything. The cream filling of the

orange flan had curdled. The bulgar wheat salad might have been shovelled straight out of a roadside grit bin. Even the salad dressing tasted peculiar. The only thing that had come out properly was Dennis's broccoli and stilton soup, and Bridie wasn't the only one to notice that that was disappearing faster than anything else.

'Where's it all *gone?*' wailed Toby.

'I expect people have eaten it.'

'But Dad made gallons! There'll be none left for tomorrow!'

Clearly, in Bridie's son's view, this would be a breach of tradition as heinous as no presents, or crackers with nothing inside them. Bridie pulled the spare trays of rejected lasagne out of the oven so they could congeal instead of shrivel.

'I can't help that, can I? It's not my fault.'

Oh, horrible, horrible! If she was glancing at her watch, how on earth did her guests feel? Bridie, at least, could scurry off into the kitchen on one excuse after another. This party was so leaden that nobody followed her. Even the very few neighbours they invited who still bothered to come, on such an awkward night of the year, to what was so obviously at root a family occasion, seemed drained of the will to break out of their drab little clusters – though it was hard to credit that they, too, were simply worn out with the effort of not mentioning Liddy.

Who hadn't come. Or phoned with an excuse. Or even sent her children along under the perfectly adequate wing of another sister. At one point, pushing the pine nuts she hated to the side of her plate, Heather had called out,

'Daisy!' as usual, and then remembered. For a moment, the silence was awful. Then everyone in the little circle pitched in at once.

'Funny about you and pine nuts.'

'Did you notice what they're doing to the overpass?'

'Aren't dogs *useful*? Harry's padding round positively *hoovering* the carpets.'

Everyone soldiered on. Bridie got more and more irritable with her sons. 'Don't put those plates down there, please!' 'No, you *can't* slip upstairs and watch telly. It's once a year!' And Dennis was singled out for simple offensiveness. 'Yes, do have another beer. Is that seven, or eight?'

'Keep your hair on. It's a party.'

'When isn't it?'

Dennis pulled shut the kitchen door and came up close. For a moment, Bridie thought he was going to slap her. But, to her astonishment, he slid his arms around her waist and tugged at her gently. 'Leave all that.'

'I'm *busy*.'

'You can't hide in here all night. Let Lance make the coffee. Come out and hold my hand while I listen to Heather going on about pensions.'

'I haven't time to——' But he'd taken her by the wrist, and pulled. And, sure enough, with him beside her it was easier. The evening ground on, through a score of stilted conversations and forced jokes. But she cared less and less. While Neil was running through his problems with the firm that put the thermostat in his hot-water tank, she suddenly had a thought. It wouldn't have killed them –

any one of them — to *insist* that Daisy and Edward were allowed to come. She was their aunt, after all. She'd had them round on Christmas Eve every year since they were born. How easily Heather and Stella could have let Liddy know this roping the children into her stubborn little sulk was just not on. A diplomatic headache for herself was quite her own affair. And George, of course, was entirely at liberty to claim he was staying by his lover's pillow to soothe her brow. But stopping the children being chased hysterically around the house by their huge cousins was quite a different matter. Bridie's mood shifted. Now sheer indifference to the fate of the evening showed on her face. Somehow the clock crawled round till everyone at last felt free to leave. Lance and Toby went off all smiles, delighted that family tradition had forced them to miss only an hour at most of other, better parties. And Bridie left the washing-up.

'Now that's not like you.'

'Everything was spoiled anyway. So why should I bother if I have to spend Christmas morning with my hands in the sink?'

She sat on the edge of the bed, fumbling with fancy buttons.

'Here. Let me.'

While he was peeling off her clothes, he heard her muttering, 'I think I hate my sisters.' But it was said in such a vague, experimental tone (like someone saying, 'I'm not really sure I like coconut,' or, 'Do you think it's too warm in here? Should I turn down the heating?') that Dennis couldn't help feeling it was almost more polite, as well as less dangerous, to choose to ignore her. Her clothes were off now, but his warm hands didn't stop. And Bridie didn't stop him. She kept up the grumbling. He surfaced to hear the words 'lily-livered' once or twice. And when he pressed her to repeat what he had taken for a muffled sexual request, he found himself having to withstand the detumescent effects of, 'What I *said* was, I'd just as soon shove their heads in a barrel as invite them to any more parties!' But drink had made her compliant. And distress gave her routine responses a fresh edge. With the result that Dennis's last party favour was good and long and deep and satisfying. And unlike the washing-up (though equally unusually), it did not on this occasion have to wait until morning.

So strange that it was Stella who let it slip.

'Oh, good!' she said, when, two days after Boxing Day, Bridie finally felt sufficiently in control of her emotions to stop by. 'You've brought back my pie dish! I've been needing that.'

'I'm sorry. I thought you had two of them.'

'Well, I did, till the other got broken at Liddy's party.'

Can a word fall and smash like crockery? 'At Liddy's party?' Bridie distinctly recalled Stella, only two weeks before, pulling the two dishes out of her cupboard and saying, 'No, go ahead. Take them both, if you like. I'm quite sure I won't need them over Christmas.'

Stella was looking horrified. Clearly, the moment the words were out of her mouth, she, too, had recalled the small interchange.

'At Liddy's party?'

Trapped, Stella did her best. 'It wasn't planned. I think it was very much a last minute thing. I'm not sure she even had time to phone round much. There was hardly anyone there. You couldn't really call it a party.'

'You just did.'

'What?'

'Call it a party. "At Liddy's party", you just said.'

'Did I?'

'Yes.'

'Well, anyway. Party. Little gathering. Whatever. She asked me if I'd help out, what with it not being planned, or anything. And I thought I'd make a couple of those asparagus and cheese tarts that look really nice in these dishes. And then, what with Liddy horsing around with George because he was smoking—'

'Smoking? George?'

Stella saw the trap open. 'Oh, only the one,' she said, tacking off desperately. But Bridie pursued her to the bitter conclusion.

'One of Heather's, I take it.'

Stella bowed her head. She was, to her credit, Bridie saw, deeply ashamed. 'Yes. One of Heather's.'

'So,' Bridie said. 'Let's get this straight, shall we, before I smash this bloody pie dish over your head—'

'There's no need for—'

'You and Heather – and Neil, presumably – went to a party at Liddy's over Christmas without even telling me.'

'Bridie—'

But Bridie was already at the door.

'Bridie!'

Bridie slammed everything on her way out. The door. The gate. The car door. And the gears.

'Bridie!'

Good job there was nothing in the street, or she'd have slammed into that as well.

'I can't *believe* that you'd be that disloyal!'

'Steady on,' Heather warned her. 'You're not the only person on the planet, you know. We all have lives of our own.'

'Look,' Bridie said. 'There's no way round this one, Heather. It was bad enough everyone letting Liddy get away with staying away from my party. But for the two of you to go to hers!'

'It was only a party.'

'It wasn't "only a party". It was a way of saying that her behaviour is acceptable. It was a way of being disloyal to me. It was a way of letting her pick on me, and isolate me from the family, and take all the blame for something we all agreed on. It wasn't "only a party"!'

'I don't know what you expected us to do.'

'I expected you to say *no*. I expected you to say, "Now listen, Liddy. It's quite unfair of you to pick on poor Bridie, and we're not falling in with it." I most certainly didn't expect you and Stella to put me and Dennis out of your minds, and just go ahead and have a good time!'

'It wasn't that big a deal, Bridie.'

'No!' Bridie screamed. 'Maybe it wasn't – for *you*. But it is for me. I'm on my own here, don't forget. Thanks to *you*.'

'You're not on your own. Don't be silly.'

'Oh, yes? Then how come I didn't get a phone call from you or Stella explaining what an awful time you'd had saying to Liddy that it wasn't fair, and if she couldn't see that either *everyone* or *no-one* was to blame, then you couldn't come to her party?'

'Bridie, are we supposed to run our whole lives around your quarrel with Liddy?'

'*My* quarrel?'

'Yes. Your quarrel.'

'I can't believe I'm hearing this,' Bridie said. 'I can't *believe* it.'

'Don't get so worked up. Don't get so upset.'

Bridie slammed down the phone. After a moment it rang, but she ignored it. When it kept ringing, she lifted it off the hook and held it away from her for a few seconds before putting her finger down to cut the connection. Then, listening for the dial tone, she laid the receiver down on the table and put a cushion over it. It was, she thought, the method she'd read about to deal with offensive calls, though, up till now, she'd never had one. She sank on the sofa. Was this why Heather had never married, because she was so unfeeling to the people around her? Was this why Miles walked out on Liddy, because her responses were so unreasonable, disgusting and cruel? Was it Stella's sheer lack of moral sense that had made Bridie despise her all these years? In short, were her family morally *bereft*? Or were they just *family*? Bridie felt like a child who'd spent her years in primary school flicking contentedly through colourful picture books entitled *Our Barnyard Friends* and *On the Farm*, showing hens with their little broods round their feet clucking contentedly in sunlit orchards, only to wake one day and realize that the truth was different, and in real life hens were kept miserably stacked in cages, their fluffy offspring routinely snatched away. She felt as if, all her life, she'd been fed certain lines. 'Blood's thicker than water'. 'The family is the strongest support'. And, like a fool, she'd bought it. She'd believed it. And it was nonsense. All of a sudden, things made sense to her – entire families torn apart by one stupid vase inherited here instead of there; brothers who lived next door to one another and didn't speak because of one unguarded word about some otherwise long-forgotten girlfriend; mothers and daughters estranged for ever because of a few sharp words about the grandchildren's manners. Before, she'd always thought, How could a silly old vase, however valuable, however long-promised, weigh against 'all that'? But if there was nothing there, if 'all that' were mere illusion, then anyone in their right mind would choose the vase. Everything looked very different when it was brought home to you that, when the chips were down, 'all that' meant nothing.

And it wasn't even as if she'd ever had an idealized view of the family. Anyone in Bridie's job knew how often it proved to be a tawdry cluster, replete with sins and miseries. There were no laws to control dangerous fathers, suffocating mothers or bullying siblings until the damage was done. Bridie had more than once found herself walking down a street in search of No. 9, or Inglenook, and realized she was imagining, behind the closed doors of No. 3, or Spinney View, far worse scenarios than the one for which she was headed, concealed behind even thicker curtains of threat, and hiding even more crippling cruelties.

Small wonder, then, that she'd so wanted to believe that it was possible to do it right. To raise a child in what Miss Minto always rather simperingly called 'the crucible of attachment'. Provide security that would see someone through the anguish of adolescence, the exhaustion of early motherhood, the loneliness of loss and the horrors of old age. The family. Somewhere to belong. Through all the commitment and training, all the case conferences, all the anxieties deep in the night, this one belief had been bedrock. Though the shape and the size of the family didn't matter, the strength of the attachments did. And these were not cobwebs, but cables; strong and lasting. They were supports to see you through.

So did it turn out to be true that, as her mother had so often observed, the tears of other people are only water? Had it been mere imagination that made her think that people weren't alone under the stars?

'A penny for your thoughts?' Dennis was in the doorway, watching her carefully.

'I was just wondering whether my sisters are shits, or if life is just shitty.'

He laughed. 'That's all?'

She nodded.

'Is it safe to come in?'

She nodded again, speechless with misery. He crossed the room and sat by her side, pulling her close. She didn't shake him off. She let him hug her.

'Families!' (It was what they'd always said about his, never hers.)

'Families!' she echoed bravely. But his had never really been what she would call a family. A few days after Dennis's birthday, a card usually came from his father (if his stepmother had remembered to remind him). The boys received money at Christmas, presumably to atone for neglect through the rest of the year. And Dennis's only brother always included in his card some apology for having forgotten everything else to do with family during the past twelve months. She could hardly remember them, really. She'd met them all, of course, mostly at weddings. And occasionally – very occasionally – there was a phone call between Dennis and Neville to bring one or the other up to date on some ailing aunt, or their stepmother's constant operations. Bridie had always presumed she'd meet them all again one day, at the inevitable funerals. But Dennis's family had never figured in their way of life. She and Dennis never left a few hours early on their way to an airport, or back from a holiday, in order to call in on one or another of them for a quick cup of tea and a sandwich. And though their various addresses and telephone numbers in the book on the desk were dutifully scratched out and written over whenever they moved, Bridie was no longer even very sure which of the houses they were living in she'd actually seen, and which of the faded and muddled impressions in her mind were of homes long abandoned by any of the Marleys. But for the cards and the rare calls, the whole pack of them might have been strangers.

No, Dennis's family wasn't a bit like hers.

'I'm going to write to her,' Bridie declared. 'I'm going to write to Liddy and tell her off.'

'Is that wise?'

'It's the only thing left. She won't speak to me, and the others won't speak up on my behalf. Unless . . .' She turned to look at him hopefully.

'No,' he said. 'Don't look at me. I'm not sticking my nose into any of this, and I mean it.'

He'd have been hopeless anyway. 'Well, then,' she said. 'A letter it is.'

'She might just send it back.' (He sounded almost hopeful.)

'She might. But if I send it from work, with an office label, she might not catch on till she's opened it. Then, even if she shovels it straight back inside the envelope and returns it, she'll know that I'll *think* she's read it.'

Dennis sighed.

'*And,*' Bridie went on, the bit between her teeth now, 'I'm telling Heather and Stella what I'm doing. I'm sending them copies, in fact. And I'm going to ask them – no! I'm going to *insist* – that they let me know what she says about it. That way, they'll know they can't wriggle out of discussing things properly with Liddy. They'll have to pull their fingers out. They won't be able to keep putting it off, and pretending this isn't really happening.'

She knew from the look on his face that he wasn't convinced she was doing the right thing. In fact, it was obvious he thought she was doing the worst thing, but didn't want to say so. Or didn't dare. But without being prejudiced about it, why should she worry what he thought? He was a man, after all, and, as she knew from long experience inside the office and out, unless a man's pride had been dented, he was usually only too prone to thinking it 'best to do nothing'. Sometimes (as with Stella's Neil) there came allied to this the deeply offensive habit of patronizing any female who disagreed. 'Let the little ladies get on with their squabbling.' But was George out of the same box? Certainly, it still didn't seem to have occurred to him that he had a role to play in making Liddy see sense. As for why Dennis was so sure things should be left as they were, she couldn't understand it. Surely he couldn't believe this horrible family snarl-up should be allowed to persist. But Bridie wasn't in the mood to delve into the reasons for Dennis's lack of support. Nothing he could say would persuade her. So why ask?

She wrote three letters in the end. The first was a howl of anguish. The second was more professional, larded with phrases like 'I do understand,' and, 'I can quite see,' and, 'clearly, from your point of view.' The third was a blast of outrage. They lay together on the desk, their pages interleaved. As Bridie gnawed at her pen, rereading, the various sentences wailed, soothed, or hissed up at her. 'I can't *believe* that, after I've been a perfectly good sister to you all these years, you're so ready to assume the very worst about my motives . . .' 'I do see how terribly painful it must be to be brought face to face, without warning, with a bit of "reality" in a new love of almost dreamlike perfection . . .' 'Liddy, you're such a cow to cut me off like this! And such an *unfair* cow! Why pick on *me*?'

Dennis poked his head round the door. 'How's it going?'

'It's not,' she lied, because she didn't want to show him any of the letters. She was disgusted with herself, with Liddy, and the world.

'Perhaps it's as well.'

'Perhaps.'

He waited a moment, but when she said nothing more, he shut the door, and a few minutes later she heard him outside the window clanking the crates of empties into the back of the car. Usually this was a signal for her to rush round the house, picking up newspapers and catalogues and magazines to add to his neat piles of paper for recycling, as he came back for the aluminium cans. But she sat tight, unwilling to leave her desk unguarded for a moment.

At last, he left. She read all three of the letters through again. What was she planning, for God's sake? Choosing by eeny-meeny-miny-mo? If any client of hers described herself going about a big decision in this way, she'd roll her eyes to heaven. But that was emotional matters for you. They weren't like your tax affairs, where everything relevant could be so easily codified and fed into a computer, ready to be spat out, certain and correct. 'What with your added weighting for this, your extra liability for that – chug, chug – we owe you X, you owe us Y, so overall, we owe you Z.' With matters of the heart, there wasn't a snowball's chance in hell of getting the weightings right, the liabilities agreed. 'You *said* . . .' (Oh, but I never meant it like that.) 'You did this!' (But you knew I only acted that way because—) 'You should have . . .' (No. That's your way of doing things, not mine.) You might as well twirl round three times in a blindfold and stick a pin, to see which letter should go in the envelope.

She read the howl of anguish through again. No, she'd be damned if she'd let Liddy know she couldn't eat, she couldn't sleep, she was in *misery* because her family life had crumbled around her. She read the professional master-piece, repelled beyond measure by the mealy-mouthed way she'd managed to stretch her understanding of her sister's feelings out to whole paragraphs so they'd appear to outweigh the bland little snippets into which she'd compressed her own justifications. She picked the blast of rage off the desk. 'Wouldn't you think, Lids, that just enough of all those self-awareness courses you've been taking for years (on Heather's money, mind, and using me and Dennis for babysitters) might have rubbed off on you? Wouldn't you think you'd at least have enough basic honesty by now to know that all you're doing is trying to stick your spoiled, stupid, lovelorn head up your arse rather than face the fact that your beloved isn't quite the matchless dream you thought? So he kept one poky little secret from you! Oh, big *deal*! And your sisters respected you enough to tell you. Well, more fools them!'

Should it be 'more fools they'? Oh, who cared? Who cared! She wasn't going to send it, was she? Not a letter like that. You don't need qualifications in social work to know that nothing, nothing in the world, goes down as badly as the truth.

With deep regret, she tore the blast of rage to shreds. The howl of anguish, almost as regretfully, went the same way. It was the mealy-mouthed, turn-away-wrath, understand-how-you-feel sick-maker that was folded in four, and sealed in the envelope, and taken straight away to the pillar box on the corner. If Dennis hadn't been due back along the road at any moment, she might have leaned against it, too, till the evening collection, just to be sure the noxious thing was taken away, and swept out of the neighbourhood, so she could put it out of mind, and sleep in peace.

Stella denied that Liddy had even mentioned it. 'Letter? She never said anything to me about any letter.'

Bridie's disbelief was evident. 'Really? But she must have got it over a week ago. Surely you've spoken to her since then. Heather said you were over there only yesterday, doing wedding stuff.'

'We talked about flowers, mostly. I took her some designs and things.'

Bridie could not have been less interested in floral displays. 'You're trying to tell me that, the whole time you were together, she never once mentioned getting a letter from me?'

'I'm not "trying to" tell you anything, Bridie. I'm just telling you. And there wasn't any "whole time" about it. I was at Liddy's for an hour at most.'

'That's not the point.'

'Other people's sides of things are never the point with you, Bridie. Have you noticed?'

But Bridie had spent a sight too much time desperately trying to work out what was running through her sisters' minds to take a gibe like this from any of them now. 'Just a moment, Stella,' she said. 'I think I hear someone at my door. Would you excuse me?'

She hung up.

Heather was more forthcoming, if not much more helpful. When Bridie pressed her bell, she came to the door with a towel still wrapped round her head. 'You've got here quick enough! It can't be half an hour since you rang.'

Tipping her head, she let the sodden towel slip to the floor, and patted her damp hair. 'I can't go out till it's dry. Where did you fancy walking, anyway? Over the common?'

'Wherever. You'd better dry it properly. It's freezing out.'

'Make us some coffee, then.'

So Bridie made coffee. The window in the kitchen was misted up. She cleared a circle, and peered through at Heather's back view: the elongated gardens of city dwellers, some prissily cared for, others neglected, but all bare and dismal in the weak winter light. 'We ought to go out a bit further,' she called through the open doorway. 'Somewhere nice.'

'The common's nice.'

Did that mean Heather didn't have much time? A lunch date, perhaps? Or someone else's husband, escaped from the Saturday shopping. Last time Bridie asked after 'Trevor the Exporter', Heather insisted that she'd sent him packing. But there was a letter from him on the bread bin. Maybe he was back, on Heather's customary grounds that keeping on with the old one was usually a lot less trouble than starting off with someone new.

Bridie carried in the coffee. 'How's Trevor, then?'

Heather was struggling into a heavy pullover with a tight neck. She shook out her hair. 'Actually, he's getting on my nerves.'

'He was last time I asked.'

'Well, it's worse now.' But clearly Heather couldn't be bothered to go into details. Gratefully, she took her coffee and switched on the hairdryer. Rather than pitch her voice over the noise, Bridie wandered off to the bookshelves. *Corporate Law. Current Tax Exemptions. Law and the Dividend. A Guide to Trusts.* And a host of other, even less appealing titles. What did she read for pleasure, for heaven's sake? She read as a child. She was never like Stella, whose bookmark barely moved from week to week. Heather was found as often as Liddy shrugging off all interruption, racing towards the end. So where were her novels now? Where were the books that shone a light on others' lives, and showed you how the rest of the world handled the illness of a child, the sudden social reverse, the grip of passion? Where were the books about birth and marriage and death?

'Are all your books about your work?'

In answer, Heather nodded to a trunk on which sat heaps of shells, and several plants. Oh, Bridie couldn't help thinking. I see! You keep your guides to tax law on the shelf, but all your guides to living out of sight, so, like your stone heart, they'll be out of mind.

She lasted about ten minutes into the walk. The moment she raised the topic, she saw the look flit over her sister's face: 'Oh, no. Here we go again.' But still she couldn't help it.

'So what did she say about my letter?'

Heather looked cross. 'We've hardly talked. I've been so busy this week.'

'But did she tell you what I wrote in it?'

Heather brushed past a clump of hawthorn, sending a shower of ice-cold droplets into her sister's face. 'She said it was a bit unfriendly,' she admitted unwillingly.

'*Unfriendly*? I think, in the circumstances, it was more than reasonable. More to the point, though, what did she think about what I *said*?'

'She didn't go into that.'

'And you didn't bother to ask her, I suppose?'

Heather was nettled. 'She did say she couldn't see why on earth you'd bothered to send it.'

'Then she couldn't have read it properly!'

'I think it annoyed her too much.' She sent another shower of freezing droplets into Bridie's face. 'From what I could gather, there was an element of unpleasant innuendo about it.'

Bridie stopped short and tugged her sister's sleeve, to spin her round. 'Be fair to me, Heather. Tell me what she said.'

Heather's gaze wandered round the dripping trees.

'All right, then. She said it was perfectly vile.'

'Vile?' Bridie felt she'd been punched in the stomach. *'Vile?'*

'That was the word she used.'

'She should have seen the two I didn't post!'

Heather said sternly, 'Maybe it was more hostile than you realized, then, if that's the way you were feeling.'

'Why do you say that? You're just taking her word for it. It would have helped if you'd bothered to ask her if you could read it yourself!'

'She says it was so horrible, she burned it the minute it came.'

'Smart of her!' Bridie sneered. 'Oh, very clever! I only wish I'd sent you and Stella copies. I certainly meant to, but I got so worked up writing it that I forgot.'

'A good thing, too! If Liddy caught you sending copies of letters around, she'd get even more paranoid.'

'Is she trying to make out that I'm getting at her?'

'Bridie, for God's sake! Life's too short. Just drop it!'

'Because that's less trouble for you?' Bridie snapped. 'After all, it's not you who's being pushed out in the cold.'

'Speaking of cold . . .'

'We're not speaking of cold, Heather! We're speaking about me and Lids! We're speaking about the fact that I'm being treated like a leper.'

'Oh, don't exaggerate.'

'How am I exaggerating? I can't come to this wedding, can I?'

'Of course you can come to the wedding.'

'Oh, yes!' scoffed Bridie. 'You really think that, in the mood she's in, Liddy's going to invite me and Dennis and the boys?'

'Stop being such a martyr. I know for a fact that Liddy intends to invite you.'

'Well, even if she does, it's only for form's sake, isn't it? She knows quite well that none of us can go.'

'Don't be ridiculous. Of course you can go.'

'She didn't come to my party.'

'That was a party, Bridie. This is a *wedding*.'

Bridie stopped in her tracks. She was trumped, wasn't she? The bitch! The cow! Oh, clever, clever Liddy! How had she done it? How had she managed to twist everything to suit herself? If she had too few brains to see how horribly unfair, how very *wrong*, all her responses had been, how had she managed with such economy of style – saying and doing almost nothing – to trap someone who was only doing her best into this dismal role? For look who Bridie had become overnight. Abracadabra! The spiteful, cantankerous Ugly Sister who spread gossip, wrote the most unpleasant letters, and probably wouldn't come to her own sister's wedding.

She wasn't going down without a fight. After a moment's thought, she said to Heather, 'I'm warning you and Stella. If you don't support me on this, if you don't get this business sorted out before the end of March—'

Heather had turned to stare.

'If the two of you go off to this wedding without me, I'll never speak to either of you again. And that's a promise.'

The look on Heather's face was quite unfathomable.

113

Without a word she set off back across the common, towards her flat. Without a word, Bridie followed her. You would have thought the vow of silence had already begun, because, even with Heather's shortcuts, it was several minutes' hard walk before the two of them reached the street. Here, each eyed the other for a moment, and Bridie thought Heather was about to speak. But she just made a little Bridie-you-are-hopeless face, so, still without a word, Bridie strode off one way, and, with a shrug, Heather went off very quickly in the other.

7

DENNIS CAME IN THE ROOM CROWING.

'I always *said* your phone calls were pure gossip. Do you realize the bill has *plummeted*? We've not had one this low in living memory!' He flapped the single sheet of paper in her face. 'I'm going to frame this,' he warned her. 'So when you're all speaking again, and it's back in the stratosphere, I never have to hear another word about "important discussions" and "complicated casework"!'

He wandered off, flapping the phone bill and chortling. Bridie gazed after him with real affection. He'd been a brick over the last few weeks. Somehow he seemed to know exactly when he could mention the great family rift, and when it was best skirted round with discretion. And he was drinking less, too. That always made life easier. (Not to mention leaving them with more money.) And, putting her distress aside, she was less rushed, more rested. She hadn't realized up till now just how much energy all these family things had used up over the years. It was extraordinary to be able to come home from work, drop on the sofa, and not think, I must phone Stella, or, I really ought to get on with those quiches for Liddy's lunch on Saturday. Now, she'd slump with her legs out, waggling the tension out of her toes, while Dennis wordlessly passed her crisps – one for every three of his – and the television blethered in front of them. She didn't watch, exactly. Dennis's serials had never been her thing. But they were certainly relaxing. Bridie remembered having read somewhere that people absorbed in the box showed less brain activity than people sleeping. At the time, she hadn't believed it. She did now.

'What about supper?'

'All done,' Dennis assured her. 'Sssh! I reckon she is going to dump him after all.'

Bridie let her eyes close. That was another thing. Since all this happened, he'd taken over most of the meals. 'You never cooked like this before,' she kept on telling him.

'I always offered.'

'I don't remember that.'

'Maybe you don't, but it's true. It's just that it always seemed so complicated. I couldn't use up this, or I shouldn't make it in that dish, because you'd need it later for something for Liddy or Stella or Heather. So I'd think, Why bother? Let her do it herself.'

'I can't believe I'd just go straight in there and cook a meal. I'm sitting here *shattered*.'

'Bad day?'

And she'd have time to tell him. There on the sofa, in between crisps, she'd tell him everything that was going on. How the injunction against Sarah's ex-client had proved useless, because the police turned a blind eye to his endless nuisance phone calls and appearances on her street corner. How poor Miss Minto had burst into tears again on finding the tell-tale crust of sugar at the bottom of her mug that proved that Terence, for the millionth time, had forgotten her pleas and her strictures. How Bridie herself had practically drifted off while some new client was droning on about her housing problems. And Dennis was, by turns, amusing and perspicacious, till Bridie could remember, for the first time in ages, why she'd been ready to stand in her flowery frock and wide-brimmed straw hat in front of the registrar, and make those promises all those years ago.

'Another crisp, Brides?'

It seemed so strange to have such quiet evenings. At first, she hadn't known quite what to do with herself. She'd brought home work, and sorted all those piles of papers on the desk, and finally posted off her letter of complaint to Parkin Electrical about the extension tube missing from the new vacuum cleaner. She'd taken Harry for a lot more walks than any dog his age could need or want, written to her godmother, and stuck down the curling cork tiles in the bathroom. She'd even rearranged the airing cupboard, setting aside whole piles of worn sheets and faded towels for Toby, who had finally given up on all his up-all-night, sleep-till-noon, unemployed flat-mates, and moved in temporarily with Lance. Everything in the house appeared slightly different somehow, now she had time to look. So when, on the way back across the room, her eye fell on the photos on the chest of drawers, instead of passing by as usual, she stopped to peer. What was so odd about them? Was it that, summer or winter, inside or out, merry or grave, they all had one thing in common: every single one of them featured one or another of her sisters? Bridie fingered her way through the frames, finding it hard to believe. But it was true. Even the photograph of their first, pretty, rented cottage had Liddy complacently installed on the lawn, raising a glass to the camera.

So what was this? A shrine to sisterhood? Lance was in there, of course, but only once, at twelve, and it wasn't a good one of him. You could see Toby in one corner of a photo of Heather leaping to return a serve, but he was somewhat blurred. And Dennis wasn't anywhere, unless that was his back behind a shot of Stella leaning over her new barbecue. Somewhat mortified, Bridie went downstairs and rooted in the cupboard under the stairs.

'What are you after?'

'The photo box.'

'Boxes.'

He left his stirring to lift them down for her. She spread the spoils around her on the floor. 'There are *hundreds*.'

'Don't look at me. You're the one who always insists on my taking the camera.'

'I'd no idea we had so many.'

'What are you looking for, anyway?'

'Nothing,' she said. 'I just felt like a change.'

And change it was. Out they all came, Heather and Stella and Liddy. And in went Lance, gawping in wonder at his first balloon, Lance staring gravely over a parapet, Lance standing shyly in his first suit at Granny's funeral, Lance in a torn shirt, polishing the car. In went Toby rolling over the carpet in his Batman pyjamas, Toby furtively stealing raspberries, Toby leaning against one of the two great pillars flanking the communal front door to his first flat. Into the last of the frames went Dennis on their wedding day, Dennis playing rounders, and Dennis drenched in sunlight, stretched out luxuriously on a bench in France.

'Good holiday, that,' he said, picking his way through Bridie's mess of discarded photographs and clumps of double-sided tape. 'Where was it? Deaumont? Deauville?'

'Deaulort.'

'Deaulort.' He sighed. 'We ought to go again. I can remember thinking how nice it would have been if we hadn't had children.'

'Dennis! It was nice anyway!'

He didn't stop to argue. He was over the photograph trimmings, and away. Bridie set her new family of faces out on the chest of drawers, and stepped back to admire them. Who needed sisters anyway? Half the world didn't even have them, and they managed perfectly well. They didn't pine.

But sometimes, out of the blue, she felt *bereft*. There was no other word. The sense of loss was quite intolerable, almost unbearable physically, a ghastly tightening of the muscles in her stomach till she could hardly breathe. It was the very worst sort of panic, with the disarray in her head and the constant swilling of options – should she have done this differently, not done that at all? – so dreadfully demanding, so downright deafening, that she could barely hear a word anyone said.

'They're in the fridge, I think.'

'The *scissors?*'

'Oh, no! Sorry! In the blue basket.'

But still she wouldn't ring. Let them ring her. Liddy would not, of course. And Heather hadn't. And Stella's silence sprang, presumably, from Heather passing on the ultimatum. Perhaps they were waiting for her to realize how lonely she was going to be if she stuck to her guns. But she *wouldn't* come to the wedding. Not without some conciliatory move from Liddy, and, till now, there'd been no sign of that. Maybe her sisters were still working on it. Though, if that were the case, they would surely have got in touch by now, if only to complain about what an uphill task it was proving. No, it seemed clear she was essentially on her own. While they were all discussing music and flowers, hats and guests, she and Dennis were reduced to studiously ignoring the bright pink invitation on the mantelpiece, neither refusing nor accepting. As with so many things from their shared childhood, it had become a matter of 'wait and see'.

'Does it worry you?' asked Dennis. And she shook her head, not really dissembling because mostly, now, she did feel a strange sort of waterlogged calm, as if she were too bunged up with unshed tears to feel a thing. She was even a little proud of herself for having seemed to take, with so little trouble, advice she'd proffered so often over the years to thwarted and miserable clients: let it go; accept that,

like the seasons, things you love can end, and there's no
getting them back by mere willing, or deserving, or
fighting, or waiting.

Because, whatever happened now, something was gone.
Something was spoiled for ever. She'd never have the
confidence again that, in a hard place, your family would
support you. And it would be easier to forgive Liddy the
anger that set this fuse alight than Heather and Stella the
sheer indifference that had let it burn.

'Why? Does it worry *you*?'

'Not going to a wedding? *Worry* me?' He looked at her
as if she were unhinged. And she couldn't help smiling.
What a comfort men were, in all their raw simplicities.
Not wear a suit all day? Oh, fine by them. They were
happier in jeans and T-shirt. Not sit and listen to
speeches? Excellent! Speeches were too like school. And
as for not fretting about family, they were your man for
that. No worries on that score. Dennis had never seemed
happier, never drunk less, as though it were not his in-laws
becoming more and more distant and irrecoverable every
week, but his anxieties. Even now, he was striding off,
whistling; and cheered by his very unconcern, Bridie
found that, for half an hour or more, she herself was
humming quite merrily.

Till, out of nowhere, back it came again. Sheer, blind-
ing rage. And for the first time in her life, Bridie could
understand the dozens of her clients who fed on hate and
relished spite. Love was so *weak*. The more you
gave, the more you had, perhaps. But what a feeble mess
it was, bubbling away softly like porridge on the boil,

ever-nurturing, ever-warming. Hate was a tower of strength, a burning pillar. Its sheer incandescent energy could power whole days of loathing, whole nights of wrath. Before, when she heard these outpourings of implacable ill-will, she had assumed that some day soon they must consume themselves, burn to soft embers and die. Now she knew better. Hate was imperishable. And never, ever, more than half done. The more you hated someone, the more you watched their every move. How often she'd heard them at it in the office. 'Oh, she pleads poverty! But she's managed to re-cover the sofa!' 'Misses us all terribly? I don't think so! I know he's been out with that new woman of his four times since Saturday. Four times!' How do they *know*, she'd wondered. Where do they find the time to lurk in ill-lit alleyways and spy through drawn curtains? Now she knew. Two Sundays in a row, she'd said to Dennis, 'I'm off for a swim now. Can I take the car?' And she'd put miles on the clock, checking on Heather's lights, and Stella's garage, and having to face the fact that, without her, the family hadn't fallen apart. They were all round at Liddy's, having good times as the wedding grew closer and closer.

And hate grew.

And spread. Now she was furious with George as well, for taking no responsibility for the misery growing around him. The man was craven. What a cheek he had! He'd moved into a strong and happy family, and now, without lifting a finger to save it, he seemed content to watch the poison spread, like one of those feeble-minded spouses who said of their gun-running, drug-dealing partners,

'Oh, that was all his business. Nothing to do with me.' But wasn't that what marriage was – one flesh, shared claims of conscience, joint accountability? What was the point of it, otherwise? When she'd first married Dennis, she was outraged by his cool habit of fiddling his tax returns. He, in return, was shocked at her standards of hygiene. 'You can't use that cloth, Bridie! I've just seen you use it to wipe up those cat hairs!' They'd grown entangled, like close trees, on so many issues. It was hardly conceivable, now, that he could say of some decision of hers, 'Well, that's just Bridie for you,' or she of him, 'That's up to Dennis.' Surely, at some point, George must look round and say, 'It was more fun when Dennis and Bridie came to everything. Can't we sort something out, Liddy? Isn't it time?' Desperate to know what they might be saying to one another about this business, she tried imagining one of their conversations. 'Sit down, Liddy,' she told the busy figure she'd conjured instantly in her mind. 'Sit down, George.' Forcing her two phantom figures to the table, she made George reach out for her sister's hand. It was so real that she could see the pallid underwater glow from Liddy's lowered ceiling light fall on his fingers. Like someone trying to dub a film screened in a language they don't understand, she didn't know where to start. All she could see was Liddy's bracelet-spinning nervousness, her evident desire to rise from the table. All Bridie's attempts to start a likely conversation off – 'What I feel, George, is . . .' 'What stops me phoning Bridie . . .' – slid into mist. No further words came. Not the tiniest hint.

But Liddy couldn't keep it up for ever. The anniversaries would be upon them soon. Always before, around the end of February, the start of March, their thoughts had turned to their parents. Stella would go on her trip to the cemetery with fresh flowers, and there'd be all the memories of that sad winter, and the times before. Surely she'd have to crack then. And what would their mother be thinking about all this, if she were here? Would she be feeling she'd failed? Or would she take the line that Bridie knew her father would have taken? 'They're all grown up now, aren't they? If they can't sort themselves out, let them get on with it. I can't be bothered.'

They'd never been like this before, that was for sure. There'd been the usual quarrels through their childhood, with hot alliances running over weeks and months in the face of particular gripes and resentments. But nothing to match this. No formal schisms. No excommunications. For that was how it seemed. Halfway through February came Daisy's birthday. And since the gift could not be handed over to Liddy as usual, Bridie found herself queuing at the post office to send off the fiendishly expensive Victorian fold-flat toy theatre that would so obviously remind the rest of them of all the torrents of fancy and amusement they'd shared since early childhood. 'Quick! Bridie's finished her play! Come and get your parts!' 'Oh, Bridie, not charades! Well, I'm not playing without another drink and more of those nice crisps.' Surely they'd pick the colourful characters on their little sticks out of the box and miss her terribly. Bridie the Director. Bridie the Ringmaster. Bridie the Leader.

Or Bossy Bridie. Off our backs at last. Good riddance to bad rubbish. Just at the thought, the tears came rolling down her cheeks, worrying each of the customers coming back from the grille, and so unnerving the woman behind the counter that Bridie could barely hear her whispered instructions to put the package on the scale. 'After the head's off, why cry over the hair?' their mother used to say. But Bridie couldn't help it. She missed the oddest things: the conversations with Heather about Liddy's drinking; the cuttings from the paper Stella used to send about firms setting up, or expanding, in case Dennis should be in the mood to make an effort and send in an application; the muttered curses on the answerphone, 'Oh, bugger! You're *still* not in. I'll try again.'

The thank-you letter, when it came, was read like runes. The writing was Daisy's neatest. Was it copied out? The length was generous. But had there been editorial control, or was it simply accidental that in a closely written side and a half, Daisy had mentioned no single member of the family, apart from herself and Edward?

'What do you think?' she asked Dennis.

'What about?'

'The letter. Is it staged?'

'Staged?'

'Did Liddy write it for Daisy to copy out?'

Dennis took Bridie by the shoulders, and shook. 'You're going loopy, Brides. Did you know that? Now say these words after me: "It doesn't *matter*."'

'It doesn't matter.'

But it did. Joan, in the office, was amazed by this. 'Honestly, Mrs Marley, you're taking all this far too hard. My brother and I haven't spoken to one another in years. I wouldn't recognize him if he sat next to me on a park bench. And I can't say I care.' And, driving home one day, Bridie caught on the radio a snatch of a voice like steel. 'Oh, none of my family are on speaking terms. None at all.' Bridie veered over to the kerb and put on hazard lights so she could chase the drifting radio waves with the fancy search button. As she honed in again on the thoroughbred tones, the interviewer was pressing. 'Is this a problem?'

The voice seemed mystified by the idea. 'No. Not at all.'

The interviewer tried again. 'But what about the children – all those cousins?'

As if this were the first time she'd ever given it any thought, the woman said wonderingly, 'That's up to them, I suppose. I can't say they seem bothered.'

The rest of the interview was swallowed up by snatches of music and someone speaking French. Bridie drove on and, once she got home, she found herself scouring the scraps of paper in the desk drawer to find the number of her son's new flat.

'Mum? What's the matter? Is it Dad?'

'Dad?'

'Sorry,' said Lance at once. 'It's just that . . .'

Bridie waited.

'It's just that . . .' He clearly found it difficult to say. 'You've never rung.'

Bridie was mortified. 'I'm sure I have!'

Had Dennis been warning them to treat her gently? Lance changed tack at once. 'Of course you have. I'm sorry.' But he was right. If she were honest, it was usually Dennis who heaved himself off the sofa once or twice a week, and muttered, 'Better check the lads are still alive, and out of gaol.' Bridie would sit, half listening, and take the phone when Dennis offered it. But to her questions, Toby or Lance would so often answer, 'I just told Dad about all that. He'll tell you.' Then, the moment the call was ended, the phone would ring again, or Dennis had wandered off, or she would simply forget.

'I was just wondering', said Bridie, 'if you missed Daisy and Edward.'

'Missed them?'

Bridie felt stupid. 'It's been weeks since you've seen them.'

'Yes?'

'Well,' Bridie snapped, 'I know they're much younger, but they are your *cousins*.'

There was a little silence. Then Lance said, 'Mum, are you feeling all right?'

'I'm perfectly all right. I was just checking on you and Toby.'

'But what *about*?'

'Daisy and Edward!' said Bridie. 'Oh, never mind!' To cover her embarrassment, she asked him hastily, 'Can you come round for supper?'

'Is there something planned?'

'No. I was just thinking it would be nice.' She trawled her memory for snippets from the last conversation overheard.

'I'd love to hear more about this new course Toby's taking, and Dad says the photo project you did for work was brilliant. Absolutely brilliant.'

'Really? Did he say that?'

Bridie embroidered. 'And I was just saying how I'd like to see it too. But we agreed that, usually when you come, everyone's about, so we never get to talk properly. And then I thought, Why not invite the boys to supper?'

'Well, why not?'

'I could get Dad to make his Christmas soup.'

'I'll tell Toby.'

She put the phone down, and her hand was trembling. On the way out of the room, she caught sight of herself in the mirror and had a shock. Her face was ruby red. What an embarrassment, what awful shame, to find you'd let neglect grow so unchecked around your sons that to invite them back to the house for supper had been as difficult as hacking through a hedge of briars.

'I just invited Toby and Lance.'

'For supper?' Dennis looked up in astonishment. Bridie shrugged. 'I just thought it would be nice. Have you got time to make your soup? Lance wanted it specially.'

Had he got time for soup? Can camels spit? He was besotted with his sons. Shoving the can of beer he'd just that moment lifted off the shelf back in the fridge unopened, he reached for the car keys.

'Leave it all to me.'

After the goodbyes, Bridie went back to stack dishes while Dennis stood like a sentry at the gate, pointing to the unlit pothole. Over his armfuls of duvet, Toby said, 'Dad *still* thinks Lance can't drive.'

Bridie jammed in the powder. 'Are you sure you'll be warm enough? The heating's been off in there all week.'

'It's got to be warmer than home.'

What an odd age it was, when 'home' could mean two such different places: the first, an ice-cold flat studded with rusty appliances salvaged from skips (apart from the state-of-the-art music apparatus), dismal, ill lit and free from all adult interference; the second, a congenial burrow fashioned over years, with every convenience and a host of things to please the eye – cosy, familiar – and presumably stifling.

Though maybe, if Clare hadn't come along with them, Lance would have stayed overnight as well . . .

'She's very nice, that Clare.'

'Don't get your hopes up,' Toby warned. 'It's still Tansy he's soft on.'

'Really?' Bridie came to the doorway. 'I thought, when he brought Clare along tonight—'

'I *knew* you thought that!' crowed Toby.

'How?'

'I just did.'

'Odd that he brought her, then . . .'

Was Toby so stuffed with food and family that he'd reverted to the candour of infancy?

'Bodyguard.'

'*Bodyguard?*'

Toby was grinning. 'Didn't you realize? When you phoned up like that, Lance had an intergalactic fit. Phoned me in a panic. "This is it! The balloon's finally gone up! Now they're telling us!" '

'I'm not sure I'm following,' said Bridie.

Toby was halfway to the stairs. As cheerful as ever, his voice floated back. 'Di*vorce*!' he said, as if to the truly slow-witted. 'Lance thought that you and Dad were going to tell us you were getting divorced. That's why he brought Clare. As a sort of bodyguard.'

Bridie sank onto the sofa. With all the insensitivity of tired youth, her son hadn't even glanced back at her.

'G'night, Mum.'

'Good night.'

She was still sitting, stunned, when Dennis ambled past. 'Coming to bed, Brides?' He held out his hand and pulled her to her feet. Gratefully, she let him. Gratefully she let him push her up the stairs, and into the bathroom.

Deep in the night, she was still lying beside him gratefully. Thinking and thinking.

8

'CAN I COME EARLY?' BEGGED BRIDIE.

Lance sounded irritable. 'No, you can't.'

'Only a bit. I promise I won't peep in the kitchen. It's just that we've found these curtains—'

'No.'

'The thing is,' lied Bridie, 'your father found them in a car boot sale, and they looked just the job to keep out that terrible draught — just through the rest of the winter. You could take them down the minute it gets warmer. Lance, you must admit there's a yawning gap over those windows.'

'I admit *nothing*,' Lance said dangerously. Was he cooking already? Were things going wrong?

'They're only *curtains*,' Bridie wailed. Beside her Dennis hissed, 'What about that extension plug?' and Bridie flapped at him to keep quiet as Lance began cracking. 'What colour are these curtains?'

Bridie glanced down at the acres of warm scarlet. 'A sort

of rich brown,' she said. (Brown sounded masculine.) 'A kind of deep, majestic maroon.'

'Maroon's *red*, isn't it?'

'There is a hint of red in maroon, yes.'

'No *flowers*, or anything?'

'God, no! No pattern, even. Just maroon.'

'All right,' Lance said grudgingly. 'You can bring them round. But I'm not promising we'll put them up.'

'Of course not. You might hate them.' She turned to Dennis with the thumbs-up sign. He muttered grumpily, 'What about that frayed wiring? That's far more important than any damn curtains.'

Bridie put down the phone. 'More people die from pneumonia than from electrocution.'

'Not at their age!' But he was wandering off to find tools he could hide in his pockets. Tools that made the drive to the flat a litany of moaning. 'I'm getting crucified by all these sharp points.'

'Take them out till we get there.'

'He might be watching from the window.'

Bridie drew up outside. 'Are we too early, do you think?'

'I'm not hanging about out here. It's far too cold for that.'

Bridie lifted the huge box of curtains off the back seat. 'You'll be even colder once you get inside. Are you *sure* there's a rail?'

'Perfectly sure, Bridie. I remember pointing it out to him the very first time I saw ice on the windows inside. "All you need is some curtains," I told him. "You've even got the rail and eyes."'

'I hope the hooks match up. Aren't children *stubborn?*'

'Not as stubborn as we are . . .'

Stubborn and cunning. When Bridie had hung the curtains and pulled them across, cutting out the bleak night as well as the penetrating rattle of icy air through the ill-fitting panes, she draped herself, at Dennis's whispered command, over the rusting fridge. But how to distract them? They were such inexpert cooks it hardly seemed fair to ask Lance about Tansy or his latest work project, or to ask Toby and Beth how they met. As Dennis's hand slid round the door at floor level, grasping for the plug, Bridie said hastily, 'I had the most upsetting case today.' Abruptly, the fridge's purr stopped, and it juddered to a halt. Bridie pressed on. 'This woman came for the first time. She has two children, four and six, both girls, and what she told me was . . .'

In front of her, Toby's new girlfriend was hovering nervously. Bridie broke off to ask, 'What can I pass you, Beth?'

'Just the butter, please, Mrs Marley.'

Bridie opened the fridge door no wider than she needed to slide out the butter. 'There. Anyway, it turns out that the elder child was all set to go on a day trip with school when, out of the blue— '

Through the hatch, she could hear Dennis muttering as he stripped the wires. Raising her voice, Bridie went on with the tale, imitating first the woman herself in her outrage, and then the woman imitating all the offensive authority figures who had clearly so provoked her on her long trail to Bridie's office. Like many of her cases, it had everything: love, hate, sex, lies, and a deep strain of criminal intent. No-one stopped chopping or stirring, but they were all listening carefully, she could tell. And then the barrage began.

'But, surely, Mum . . .'

'Couldn't you . . . ?'

'I thought . . .'

'Isn't it illegal . . . ?'

She parried each question. 'The problem with doing things that way . . .' 'In government guidelines, you see . . .' 'You *can* tackle it like that, but then another problem arises . . .'

Now Lance was pointing with his knife. As he explained what bothered him most about Bridie's story, Dennis's hand crept round the door again, like pink-legged, hairless vermin. The fridge shuddered back to life under Bridie's arm, but she barely noticed, explaining as she was to Lance just how it was that her department had been left with such unsatisfactory options. Toby interrupted by pushing filled serving dishes into their hands, and Bridie followed Lance into the living room, still talking. Dennis was standing innocently by the windows, apparently admiring the curtains. And but for the tell-tale bulge back in his trouser pocket, no-one would ever have suspected that his parental instincts, like hers, had been so recently out of control.

'Shall we sit down?'

To Bridie's astonishment, Beth said a grace before they started eating. And maybe it worked some sort of civilizing magic over her sons, because from the soup to the

134

pudding they were solicitous and charming. Lance made it clear he'd never realized his mum had such an interesting job. Toby insisted on pointing both of the heaters in her direction. And Beth served skilfully and kindly, heaping more roast potatoes onto Dennis's plate than refried beans, and sensing early that Bridie's eyes were on the green vegetables rather than the Mexican Scramble. As Bridie said tipsily on the drive home, if they hadn't been her own sons, she'd have thought them *delightful*.

'But they're always like that,' said Dennis. And Bridie sighed, staring out through the drop-mottled windscreen into icy black night. All through your life you heard it. 'You can't do two things properly at once.' Well, fair enough, perhaps, if you were trying to add columns of figures and listen to the words of a song. But paying attention to both sides of your family? Was that impossible too? If you were busy worrying about things like Stella feeling left out again, or getting the salads ready for Heather's special birthday lunch, did that mean it had to pass you by when boyish bolshiness turned into maturity, and a husband started drinking out of loneliness and boredom?

'Do you want me to drive?'

He stared at her. 'We're nearly home now, Bridie. And you're *smashed*.'

'Am I?'

'I think so.' As if to prove the matter to his complete satisfaction, he took advantage yet again, propping her up as she stumbled out of the car, fetching her water as she made her way rather unsteadily up to the bedroom, then peeling off her clothes and hiding her nightie and face cream. 'You won't be needing those tonight.'

'I'm not sure I'm up for this, Dennis.'

'You'll be fine. Just remember to keep your eyes open.'

So she did. It stopped the dizziness, certainly. But it was also strange. Dennis looked different with his grave, distracted face hovering over hers, looking but not looking, attentive but miles away, focusing totally while he let go.

'Do you love me?' she asked him.

'You know I do. I always have.'

'Not always,' she admonished, squiffy enough to think a reference to the years before they met merited some rebuke.

'Ah, yes,' he admitted. 'There was that, of course.'

'What?'

'Clever,' he said, turning her over. 'Trying to catch me out.'

'Do you wish I was Beth? Or Tansy?'

'Don't forget Clare.'

'Clare, then. Do you wish I was Clare?'

'You're putting me off,' he said. 'You're making me feel old. It used just to be Heather or Stella or Liddy.'

'Well, *do* you?'

'If they're quieter in bed.'

She giggled. 'Remember Liddy through that wall in Weston-super-Mare?'

'Bridie, I'm giving you the yellow card.'

She risked shutting her eyes, and nothing drastic happened. Had she worried about Dennis and her

136

sisters? Had the joke started out of some insecurity to do with introducing the man you love to younger, prettier versions of yourself? She'd never been anxious about Stella, that was for sure. Stella's small, bloodless heart did not encompass risk and passion and stained sheets. He could have laid siege to Stella's doorstep for a thousand years, and not a shred of pity would he raise. She'd just step over him to go out shopping.

What about Heather? No. There, too, she could honestly say she'd never been worried. If Heather had been interested at the start, things might have been different (what with her specializing, as she did, in other people's husbands. What could have been more convenient?). But his contempt for Heather's selfishness had grown and grown, and showed no signs of being bitter fall-out from some short-lived affair, or scornful dismissal. Dennis was fascinated by Heather. But it was the fascination of a zookeeper for some merciless creature safe behind bars. It was the sort of open-mouthed marvelling earned by anyone determined and insensitive enough to batter their way through other people's feelings to the top. 'I couldn't love you. But I love to watch.'

And what about Liddy? From the first day they met, he'd been little short of fatherly to her. He'd fixed her dripping taps, and set her window boxes more firmly on their ledges, and moved her in and out of flats just as he did now with his own sons. And Liddy had sat back and teased. 'As soon as you've done that, Denny . . .' 'While you've got the wrench out . . .' 'Since you're here . . .' Things only changed a little after Miles, in that the two of them worked as a team. But it was always Dennis who lifted his head from the cupboard under the sink to declare which of the pipes was the problem and what must be done, or made the decision whether the lawnmower was worth one more service. Indeed, it was Dennis who ran Liddy to the hospital for Daisy's birth when Miles was away in the Gulf, and Dennis who sat beside her answering husbandly questions and doing husbandly things till Bridie got back from her conference and took over. When Liddy's lovers left (before and after Miles), it was Dennis who mopped her, and cheered her and cajoled her. Had Dennis loved her? Well, of course he had. But it was the way you love another woman's child – generously, easily, free of the rules and the problems. Dennis loved Liddy the way that everybody loved her. How could that worry Bridie? Only the sick at heart are ever jealous of a child.

'What about you, then?'

'Sorry?'

'Bridie! Have you fallen *asleep*?'

He didn't bother offering again, or asking what was on her mind. He just rolled off and started struggling into his pyjamas. 'Strange meal. I loved the celery bake thing, though I must say that I didn't take much to that Mexican Tumble.'

'Scramble.'

'Odd to be vegetarian and Christian, don't you think?'

'Everyone that age is odd.'

'Still, it's strange to think that one of these girls is going to be family one day.' He punched the pillow. 'I'm going to sleep now, Bridie. So when you suddenly realize what you've just missed, wake someone else.'

'I'll do that, Dennis.'

'Good.'

He switched sleep on like a tap. His snoring rose. For once the noise didn't bother her. For quite a while she didn't even make the effort to push him over to his quiet side. She just lay thinking. He was right. It was so strange to think that two unknown girls like Beth and Tansy would some day soon be drawn so deeply into their lives that their joys would be shared unreservedly by herself and Dennis, and all their sorrows would be griefs of theirs. That was the trade-off, when you came to think. You fell in love, and as a part of the deal you got a second shelter from the storm. More people to whom you mattered. More people who, after you'd flown off on holiday, would find their hearts stopping when they heard the words, 'Reports are coming in . . .' And, in return, fresh doors to distress would open all around you. Would this young Beth or Tansy be crying at Dennis's funeral because he'd been so kind, and, oh, his grandchildren would miss him so? And would she weep when she saw Bridie in the nursing home, wittering and drooling? 'She was so good to us. Do you remember those brand-new lined curtains she insisted on putting up to keep us warm that first winter? "Maroon," she kept saying. "From a car boot sale!"'

The snores grew louder. Bridie gave him a heave, then tucked herself closely beside him to stop him rolling back. All night she dreamed of gauchos and campfires ('That's that Mexican Shamble,' said Dennis in the morning), and even before the first of her clients came shuffling dispiritedly through the door, she was flicking through the work diary, wondering which was the best weekend to invite all four young people – five, if Clare wanted to come along – for a walking weekend at Miss Minto's frequently offered empty cottage in the borders.

That's when the capital letters sprang off the page. LIDDY'S WEDDING. Her heart stayed steady, though. It was unhurried consideration, not some horrible jumble of feelings, that made her keep turning back the pages. How about the weekend before? No, that was the Saturday she'd promised Terence she'd take the in-service training. The weekend before that? No, that was no good, either. Bridie turned back another page and suddenly there it was – yesterday's staff meeting, and along with it, on the same page, already gone, unnoticed, unremarked, two ringed dates: 29th February and 4th March.

The anniversaries.

How could it possibly have happened? Sarah was passing through the room. 'What's the date?' Bridie asked casually, as people do. 'It's the seventh,' said Sarah. 'No, it's not. It's the sixth.'

But there had really been no need to check. Bridie had known the moment she'd peeled the double page apart. After all, Mrs Carter had come in on the Monday. The Council meeting about travellers was midweek. And there was her reminder to herself to get the work appraisals in to Terence by Monday 9th at the latest.

But she had missed them. Totally. She hadn't given them a thought. And Dennis had said nothing. Had Stella gone, as usual, with the flowers? She hadn't rung – the answerphone was working perfectly. Had she just gone ahead with something they did every year, and cut Bridie out as if she no longer existed? And how come neither of the other two had taken Stella to task, or tried to make amends? Even if Liddy was in no mood to let her icy heart melt, surely it wouldn't have killed Heather to ring and say, 'What about Wednesday, Bridie? I'm not sure what Stella's doing about the flowers, but shall we go together, you and I?'

But Bridie hadn't noticed. That was the astonishing thing. The red-flagged days had slid by in the usual flurry of little fusses. Harry's trip to the vet for his mange spots. The funding panic from on high when one of the assessors scrambled his reading of the quarterly accounts. Miss Minto's millionth tearful resignation. Admittedly, it had been a busy week. Still, not to notice. Not to even *notice*.

She couldn't help it. She sat wreathed in smiles.

Dennis, of course, thought very little of it. 'Well, yes,' he said. 'I sort of half noticed, if you see what I mean.'

'You can't half notice something like that,' said Bridie. 'Either you did or you didn't.'

'Well, I did.'

'But you didn't say anything.'

'Nothing to say, really, was there?'

Bridie wiped down the draining board, and draped the cloth over the tap. What a lot she was learning about things she'd always thought she understood. She had, for example, believed that the close links in her family were real. And now she'd found that she and her precious sisters were just a group of disparate souls with a shared start, whose running intimacy was based on nothing more than her own determined pushing. For years, it now appeared, she'd been stage-managing these people, giving them parts to play and making them perform, just to fulfil some strange need of her own, and illustrate a false belief. She'd really thought that love and care could guard and preserve things. What was that prayer from school? 'The Lord love and keep you.' Well, maybe He could, but clearly Bridie couldn't. When she was young, she'd gone to San Francisco with a friend and seen a poster of a glistening horse pounding over the prairie. 'If you love something,' the words said, 'let it go. If it comes back, it is yours. And, if it doesn't, it never was.' Her girlfriend had bought three: the perfect presents to tuck inside her 'Frank Zappa In Concert' poster roll. But Bridie was warier. There had been something about the message she hadn't liked. Was it, she wondered now, the thought that one's flesh and blood could, if they chose, canter away without warning? Hadn't her whole life, including her life at work, been somehow designed to stop the members of families being hurled out, all by themselves, like atoms into black chaos?

'Perhaps they were doing a test run for the wedding,' Dennis said.

'Test run?'

'To see if you'll crack at the last minute.'

'I wondered that. When I first opened the diary and realized, that's what I thought: Perhaps they're just checking to see if I'm serious. But then I thought, They've had two days since then.'

'Perhaps Heather will phone this weekend.'

'Perhaps she will.'

But Bridie didn't think so. If anyone was going to ring, they'd have done so already. The only question now was why they hadn't. The casual reasons – 'been a bit busy recently', 'no, it can't have been that long, surely' – would have had to have been jettisoned after Wednesday's trip to the cemetery. Only the serious reasons were left to them now: anger, bitterness, crushing embarrassment, even fear. But underlying every one of these had to lie something else, surely. Something so massive, wide and profound that it could weigh heavily enough in the scale to stop each one of them from picking up the phone, or coming round.

Sheer bloody indifference. That was what.

9

WHEN EVERYONE HAD PULLED THEIR CHAIRS INTO THE
circle, Terence began with an update on the child from
the Turner Street fire, and they all tried not to look at Miss
Minto as she sententiously intoned, 'God setteth the
solitary in families,' her habitual response to any successful
placement.

'Perhaps God should think twice,' muttered Bridie.

Terence laid down his pen on the agenda pad. 'Oh,
Bridie,' he sighed. 'I hope you're not going to stay in this
mood all through the meeting.'

'Sorry.'

'No, really,' Terence persisted. 'It does make it difficult
for everyone in the group.'

As if she didn't know. The job was hard enough, and
fighting cynism in your colleagues could be exhausting.
She'd never been more relieved in her life than when
Mrs Hooper gave up on young people entirely, and
retrained for nursing-home liaison. (Unless it was when

Georgia Hunt gave up entirely and slammed down her resignation.) Everyone had periods of burn-out. Some people moved sideways, some into administration, and some out. But during the weeks they were coming to the decision, everyone suffered horribly.

'Sorry,' she said again. But maybe because it wasn't a long agenda on his lap, and they'd begun on such an up-beat note, Terence pursued the issue. 'Is there a problem, Bridie?'

Bridie inspected her fingers.

'Bridie's fed up with families,' Sarah explained. 'This business with her sisters is getting to her.'

Bridie shot Sarah a resentful look. She hadn't confided in her colleagues so they'd feel free to bring her problems up in group. Not that she'd told them the half of it. She'd talked freely about the rising sense of tension as the days ticked away. And she'd had quite long discussions with one or two of them in the little galley kitchen about what could be reasonably expected from close relations in the way of emotional straight-dealing. But she had never said a word about how this business was slowly but surely poisoning her work life. She'd had her problems with the job before, of course. Everyone did. Each case was a series of frustrations and setbacks, and at times the pressures were so intense that it was impossible to do anything properly. Then there were the added irritations of ceaselessly unfurling policy change. Bridie had sat in a hundred meetings, scoring her pad savagely each time some project manager came out with the phrase of the moment: 'progress chasing', 'volunteer linking', 'access management', 'community resourcing', 'support facilitation'. All of them still made her growl. But the words could change all they wanted. Always the principle remained the same. The poor could not be given a penny more than the worst paid of workers; anything else would be a bounty on indolence and vice. And if the unemployed and job-shy could stay alive on their mean pittances, then surely so could the others: the old, the sick and the downright incapable. Bridie had had to sit with an impassive face as each approach brought in its own creeping terminology: 'community empowerment', 'client advocacy', 'targeted care packaging', 'mutual network support'. It would still boil down to water seeping down filthy walls, distressed and watchful children, vermin, cold and despair. Easy, in all this, for anyone to misunderstand what it was that was actually upsetting them. Bridie would see a new name on her list. 'Mrs Henrietta Wilkes. Widow. (82) Outside concern.' She'd visit for the first time, admiring the plaster dogs along the mantelshelf, the flourishing plants in the brass pots, the framed, embroidered pictures of cottage gardens. In the front room would stand the old cabinet radio that still worked 'on the foreign', and the natural stone fireplace put in by Eric, Mrs Wilkes's late husband. All that was wrong was that her grocery money had gone astray, not for the first time, and Mr Patel from the corner shop had thought someone from social services might be able to sort out something to curtail the increasingly frequent drain on his charitable instincts.

And so began the long, long, downward trail, through broken trains of thought and unwashed hair, to semi-starvation and ineradicable suspicion of the people in the next flat. Bridie could deal calmly and professionally with the delayed assessments and the mislaid paperwork. She could be patient with the callous relations and indifferent neighbours. She rose above Hetty's stubborn last-minute refusal to move into the sheltered accommodation that had taken whole weeks to arrange, and even managed to keep her temper with the ambulance attendant who, after the first serious fall, managed to lose, on a drive of less than five minutes, the only photo Hetty still had of Eric in uniform. The rage only began when Hetty was moved out to a nursing home, where the uncaring staff dosed her half out of sentience, and the television was kept blaring so loud that even the deaf couldn't think. How fast the months went after that. It hardly seemed a moment before the skin on Hetty's legs was red, raw and peeling. 'But that's the problem, isn't it, if they don't walk? And if they can't go outside, where else is there? Bedroom to sitting room. Dining room and back. It's not much, is it?' And, to be fair to the staff, Hetty was awkward about leaving her room, embarrassed by the pads they'd expected her to wear since the regular 'accidents' started. The lady in the other bed got on her nerves, wringing her hands all day and begging to be allowed to go home, where everyone, she insisted, was 'waiting for me, worried sick about where I might be'. But even she was better than the woman Hetty had been paired with before, who wailed all night, and kept taking Hetty's ill-fitting teeth out of the glass and shoving them into her own mouth. Bridie stared bleakly at the signs on the wall. 'Today is WEDNESDAY'. 'The month is APRIL'. 'Our next meal is LUNCH'. None of the rest of it was a surprise. Only the speed. A mere two months until the transfer to the long-stay hospital, and then the usual claim, 'She's so distressed. We think she might be hearing voices now. The tranquillizers will be helpful.' One more week to the bladder infection that 'wouldn't respond', and the message on Bridie's desk when she got back from her refresher course on juvenile referral only a day after the funeral. 'If I'd not stayed on for the workshops . . .' she'd said to Dennis. And he'd just shrugged. A client is a client.

Bridie drove past Mrs Wilkes's old flat no more than a week after the file was closed. The windows had been repaired, the woodwork painted. Even the guttering had been replaced. Bridie got out of her car, and peered through the freshly washed windows. No faded and peeling wallpaper now, of course. How else would the confident 'SOLD' have been slapped over 'FOR SALE' in such a short span of time?

And then the rage boiled over till she could almost hear the voices in her own head. 'Who do you want to blame, Bridie? Take your pick. The family? The neighbours? The ambulance attendant? That careless short-stay home? The hospital? Or that last horrible ward at Manley Heath?' But part of the job is knowing when your personal fears are spilling over. You see the boundaries crumble; but with reports to write, and fresh decisions to be made, it is important to work out if it was the crappy, underfunded system not doing its job, or simply Creeping Old Age and Death routinely, calmly, doing theirs.

And there'd been other misplaced angers, too. The sheer despair of seeing misery breed misery, failure spawn failure, till she could have gone mad with the fear (unsayable, impossible to share) that one day these hard-faced, grasping children of deprivation might take over the world, outnumbering children like her own, who had been raised on cushions of sufficiency, expecting to be able all their lives to lean on such staples as justice and empathy. Was there a future in which they took over, these marauding gangs, with their rushes from boredom and their ceaseless destructive cravings? Certainly they seemed hydra-headed: each time she studied her casebook there were more. So why not cut her losses and run and hide, turning her face from this simmering misery? Simply protect her own?

But these were fears born of overwork and failure. A few good nights' sleep, a few days' leave, and she'd return to work a different person, ready to wrap a case up in an afternoon, lean on an awkward official, even stage a fit of outrage to get her way, and change a life. Those were the days she thought it was all worthwhile. She'd see the tears of relief when the wheelchair came back mended, the debt was cancelled, the bedding handed over, and she'd know she had made a difference. Someone was better off some-how, and right now. And this was what kept them all going. Look at Miss Minto's triumph about the Turner Street child. God setteth the solitary in families, and families can be helped.

So what could be worse than doubting the family? Hard enough to get out of bed in the morning and come to work if you thought it was Miss Minto's 'crucible of attachment'. Downright impossible if you suspected it was a waste of space. She felt like someone who'd faithfully kept their parachute in good repair, then tugged the cord in an emergency to find it didn't even bother to open. Why spend your life shoring up families, if families don't work? And hers was supposed to be the best kind, after all. A textbook example. Almost a prototype. Practically a joke! And it had proved useless. *Useless*.

'Bridie?'

They were all staring at her once again, and Bridie suddenly realized that this week's uncluttered agenda was no accident. Usually, if there were few cases on a rolling boil, the meeting was gratefully shelved. But clearly there'd been some discussion behind her back. This space had been cleared for her. She was expected to explain.

She took a breath.

'I am a bit rattled. But, really, it's nothing. I will get a grip.'

'It must be horrible, though,' Len pushed out the boat. 'I can see why it's so difficult.'

'When is this wedding?' asked Terence, pretending he didn't know. 'Is it next week, or the week after?'

'It's on the twenty-seventh,' Bridie said. And she burst into tears.

'There!' Sarah crowed, thrusting the box of tissues into Bridie's hand. 'I told you all that she was in a terrible state. She's up and down like a bride's nightie.'

'Sarah!'

Sarah placated Miss Minto as best she could. 'I'm sorry. But it's true. She can't do her job properly. If you so much as say the word "family" to Bridie now, she practically spits in your eye!'

'I'm sure I'm not that bad,' snivelled Bridie.

'Yes, you are. You're *awful*. Even Dennis keeps phoning up to worry about you.'

'I didn't know that.'

'Bridie,' said Terence, 'shall we stop this now? Or are you ready to talk about it a little? If you think it will help.'

Bridie snuffled and wiped. 'I certainly hadn't realized that I was making things so difficult for everyone . . .'

'You're *not*,' said Sarah. 'We're just *worried* about you.'

Bridie took another fistful of tissues. 'I'm furious with myself. I know I'm being stupid, and just because my family's suddenly being horrible, that's no reason to turn against families in general. But I can't help it. I feel terrible.'

'And we can't have that,' said Terence, clearly meaning it not only personally, but professionally as well. 'So what about it, Bridie? Can we have a little stab at it?'

'My family?'

'If you don't mind.'

'What, now? In the group?'

'How about it? We could work through the issues and see if we could find a way out. Fresh eyes, and all that. It might just help. And it would be a great relief to have you back on form. We're missing you.'

Bridie looked dubious. 'I've talked about it over and over,' she said. 'And not just to Sarah. You all know what's going on.'

'I thought we might role-play a little,' Terence said airily.

Bridie was horrified. She turned straight to Patricia, fresh back from yet another bloody course. Patricia stared up at the ceiling, apeing innocence.

'*Role*-play?'

'Come on,' Terence coaxed her. 'What have you got to lose? If we end up stamping on your shadows, we'll knock it off at once, and that's a promise.'

'All right,' said Bridie, feeling she had no choice, and understanding for the first time in her life just why so many of their clients hated their guts.

Somehow Patricia took over, as Bridie had known she would, pompously eliciting only 'the bare facts' out of Bridie, and scolding her every time she embellished them with any feeling. 'Don't, Bridie,' she kept saying. 'You'll prejudice the players.' Sarah kept faith in her way, rolling her eyes to heaven whenever Patricia interrupted, and squeezing Bridie's hand behind the chair in covert sympathy. But she still took the role of Liddy with alacrity when it was offered, Bridie couldn't help noticing with a quick shaft of bitterness. Miss Minto agreed to be Stella. There was a brief kerfuffle between Terence and Patricia over the virtues of protagonists taking their own roles, which Terence lost, so Bridie had to be herself, or make another fuss.

'And Len, you're Heather.'

'So did I get an invitation, then?'

'Even Bridie got an *invitation*,' Sarah reminded him sharply. 'The problem is that, what with her sisters not even being in touch, Bridie can't go.'

'*Feels* she can't go,' Patricia corrected her.

Bridie dissolved into floods, from sheer humiliation. Never again, not ever, would she question her clients' judgements on what they could, and couldn't, do. Not yet in character, Miss Minto leaned forward and patted her on the knee. 'I am so sorry, dear. So very sorry.'

'Shall we get started?' said Terence.

Patricia turned to Len. 'Heather,' she asked him. 'Why don't you start us off. What's your line on this business?'

Instantly, Len passed the buck. 'I think it's going to be a really big deal for this family if Bridie doesn't come. So I'm asking you one last time, Liddy. What's the real reason you won't invite Bridie to your wedding?'

'I *have* invited her,' Sarah responded. 'If she doesn't choose to come, that's her problem.'

'How can she come if she knows you're so cross you won't even speak to her?'

'You're not really speaking to her, either. Nor is Stella.'

Clearly, this sort of family bickering came all too easily to Len and Sarah. Impatiently, Terence turned to Miss Minto. 'Let's bring you in on this, Stella. Why aren't you talking to your sister?'

Miss Minto took so long that Terence gave up on her. He turned back to Len. 'Well, Heather, you haven't been in touch either. What's your beef?'

Again, Len fudged, turning to Bridie. 'You know me best. Why won't I make an effort to sort things out?'

Bridie just shrugged.

'You must have *some* idea. What am I thinking?'

'Honestly,' Bridie said, 'I can't begin to think what might have got into you. It's not as if you're frightened of Liddy. Quite the opposite. You've certainly never bothered before to fall in with what she wants. And at the start you seemed to be perfectly reasonable. Then, after we told Liddy, it all fell away.'

'But why did *I* take it so badly?' Sarah interrupted. 'Do you think I really believe I might be marrying a child abuser, and I don't want to know?'

And suddenly they were into it. Bridie let them be. They made enough jokes as they went through to lift her spirits and, after a while, they barely needed her to correct them, pulling up one another for getting events out of order, or momentarily forgetting the names of their partners or children. It was both comfort and amusement to watch the way that every single tack they took bogged down again and again in the mire of making no sense at all.

'It *can't* be that. If I'm tough enough to run a bank, or whatever it is I do, then surely I'm tough enough to tell you when your head's stuck up your arse.'

'I really can't work out why, after all these years, I'd suddenly start acting this way.'

'I don't see how things are better for anyone with me taking sides like this.'

'I can't *imagine* what I'm thinking here.'

Each validation of the sheer mystery of it all cheered Bridie more. Finally, Terence cracked.

'So what the hell's clogging the works?'

'*I* don't know,' Bridie said. 'I've thought and thought. And I can't think of *anything*.'

'Could that be it, then, dear?' Miss Minto said. 'Could it be something you don't know?'

'What do you mean?'

'Well, only that.'

'In my own family?'

'It happens,' Terence said gently.

They all sat, carefully not watching, as Bridie thought. Could Miss Minto be right? Could there be something she didn't know that had such a bearing on the issue in hand that it had derailed everything? Was Liddy perhaps pregnant, unable to face any pressure to reverse her plans? Or did George secretly loathe social workers with such a passion he couldn't bear one at his wedding? But even the most outlandish of scenarios couldn't explain why Stella and Heather were colluding with this. Nothing made sense of it. Nothing.

'Something in the past, perhaps?' Miss Minto was prompting vaguely. 'Something that happened a long time ago?'

'What *sort* of thing?'

Now Patricia was on the bandwagon. 'Didn't you tell us Liddy's husband as good as vanished overnight? Is it just possible that he has something to do with this?'

'I don't think so,' said Bridie. 'I mean, we never even talk about Miles any more. He isn't really mentioned.'

'Odd that, though,' said Sarah. 'For your family.'

Bridie fought rising panic. 'I suppose it is.'

'I wonder,' said Patricia, failing to disguise her growing excitement at this fresh tack. 'I wonder if this telling Liddy business hasn't perhaps raised echoes of things that nobody told you then.'

'And still isn't telling you.'

They were all running with it now.

'You inadvertently let a "child abuse" cat half out of the bag, and she closes down on you totally.'

'Can't talk about it. Rather not even see you.'

'And the other two obviously sympathize with the depth of her feelings enough to go along with her, however much they can see it hurts Bridie.'

'And this Miles fellow just cleared off one day . . .'

'Very suspicious.'

Shut up! thought Bridie. Shut up! Shut up! You are *disgusting*, all of you. You see it *everywhere*. Dennis is right. You are the new Gestapo!

But all she said was, 'Aren't you jumping a little to conclusions?'

'What was he like, though?'

Bridie thought back over the five flown years, and said determinedly, 'He always seemed a very nice bloke to me.'

'That's *exactly* what you used to say about George!'

Oh, how she hated them! Now here was Patricia trying to imply that Bridie was a hopeless judge of character. But she would not be riled by accusations of naivety. She would not! Ever since she was a child, she'd been beaten with that stick. What was so wrong with assuming people's characters were good, and their motives well-meaning? Whatever the canny may claim, to trust others isn't stupid. Her mother may have had a deep contempt for this way of going through life ('The innocent are *blind*'), but maybe just because this tireless, unsleeping suspicion had so repelled her, her daughter would be damned before she'd start regretting that finding people out for perfect shits came, each time, as a cold surprise. And Miles *was* a decent bloke. *And* an honourable father. It was the worst shock to Liddy when he'd shot off back to the Gulf like that, never phoning, never writing, and barely even staying in touch with the children, tiny as they were, except for the cheques and the presents, and the occasional soppy card. Liddy could never even speak of it. 'Please don't!' she'd say, when Bridie tried worming Miles back into conversations, or asking after him, or even just mentioning him to his own children. 'Bridie, just leave it, would you? Can we please talk about something else?'

'But, Liddy. It may not matter quite so much for Edward, perhaps. But Daisy *remembers* him. You really mustn't—'

'Just shut up, Brides!' And *slam!* would go the nearest door, leaving her niece and nephew so much more upset than any mere increase of distance from a father one barely knew, and the other rarely mentioned. So after a while Bridie had shelved the working principle 'one child, two parents' just to keep the peace, the same way she always ran up the white flag about the Fletchers' son being 'a bit of a daydreamer' instead of 'autistic' if she wanted to get anywhere in the ensuing conversation, or chose her tenses carefully when she was talking to Harriet Macrae about the husband who 'must have wandered off with amnesia' along that cliff path fifteen years ago. She felt her stomach knotting. Could it be guilt? Had she perhaps been negligent in not persisting in trying to keep Miles 'alive' for Daisy and Edward over the last five years? But she had honestly done her best. And it wasn't as if he was totally forgotten. The cards and presents still came. There were even, according to Heather, occasional visits. And certainly Neil and Stella always seemed to know which company he was with now, and what his salary prospects were, and when he'd next be coming through the duty-free. So she'd been happy just to let it lie. It wasn't as if he'd been wiped off the planet, after all. He'd simply managed to slip out of mind. Even Dennis, who'd been so close to him, under car bonnets, over blocked sinks, up on leaking roofs, never even mentioned him.

'Is that all, Bridie?'

She dragged her attention back to them. 'All?'

'Is that it? Just, "he was a nice bloke"?'

'He *was* a nice bloke.'

Len grinned at Bridie. 'Just like Dennis, then?'

'Dennis?' Her tone was shrill with misgiving. 'What's Dennis got to do with any of this?'

As if to order, Len's grin vanished. 'Nothing,' he said, embarrassed. 'It's just that that's what you always say about Dennis, too, if anyone asks. That he's "a nice bloke".'

'Dennis . . .' Patricia turned to Terence. 'Why did we miss him out, do you think?'

'Miss him out?'

'In the role-play.' Spotting a way through to trying the somewhat discredited technique again some time in the future, Patricia pursued her point. 'It's hardly any wonder we didn't get anywhere if we ended up missing out one of the principal players.' But Terence wasn't listening. He was staring across the circle.

'Is Bridie going to *faint*? She looks quite *ashen*.'

Patricia's gaze followed his. 'Bridie? Did you just think of something? Is it what I said?'

Oh, God! The woman was a positive bloody *ferret*. Bridie had faked faints before, back in her primary school, when things got desperate. Dare she do it now?

'Bridie?'

'Catch her, Neil! Quickly!'

'Bridie!'

So Mother was right. The innocent are blind. And deaf. And stupid, too.

So stupid.

Dennis.

Mystery solved.

10

DEVILS CAN LIVE IN VERY QUIET PONDS – THAT WAS ANOTHER
of her mother's. And, once again, it's possible that Mother
was right. Because when Heather finally got in touch
again, a week before the wedding, overflowing with
apologies ('I am so sorry, Bridie. We have been trying.
We've tried every *day*. But Liddy won't give an *inch*!'),
there was no need for Bridie to fake her calm, indifferent
answer. As soon as she'd swallowed her mouthful of toast,
the words came out naturally.

'Don't worry. It doesn't matter.'

Christ, she thought, catching in her own voice an echo
of Heather's customary lack of concern, we might be *twins*.
But this time Heather could not have sounded more fretful
and anxious. 'It's *not* all right, Bridie. Don't pretend it is.
Stop being brave, and talk to me.'

Bridie looked longingly at her cooling egg. 'I've
nothing to say, I'm afraid. I'm tired of the whole business.
So is my family.' How strange, she thought, slipping a

tiny bit more toast into her mouth, to let drop the oh-so-familiar little word, and suddenly have it mean a whole different constellation of faces. 'In fact, we're thinking of going off to France a week on Sunday for a little break. We thought we might take Lance and Toby and the girls, and—'

'*France?*'

'Deaulort,' said Bridie. 'Dennis rather liked it when we were there before.'

'But what about, you know' – Heather was floundering – 'next Saturday?'

'I'm sure you'll all have a lovely time,' Bridie said, and added spitefully after a moment, 'What with Stella's nice floral displays, and the well-thought-out sandwiches.'

'I mean, about what you *said*. That if we go to the wedding without you, you'll never speak to either of us again.'

'Oh, that!' said Bridie. 'Oh, yes.' She lifted another spoonful of egg. 'Well, that still holds.'

'Bridie,' warned Heather. 'Don't you dare go out. I'm coming round right now.'

'What, leaving the office, Heather? During work hours?'

But Heather missed that one. She'd just hung up.

While she was waiting, Bridie cleared the table and loaded the dishwasher. One of the things she'd really loved about the last few days was the ethereal sense she had of floating through her life, as if she were almost hanging over herself, watching, like some dispassionate third party. The shock had made everything vivid. Saucepans and taps and houseplants suddenly had harder edges, as if the air around them had been stilled. It was, thought Bridie, a bit like the feeling people describe before they faint (if they aren't fakers). All of her actions were slower, more deliberate. It would be like this after someone died, she kept on thinking. Each moment would feel special. 'This is the way I fetch the milk in, now I am alone.' 'This is the way a widow plumps her pillow.' 'This is how someone whose life is ruined walks down their garden path.'

Dennis and Liddy. What a joke! Who would have thought she could have missed it? It was so obvious, what with Miles shooting off like that without a word, and Dennis wandering round all battered and uninterested in everything. She couldn't remember all that much – just enough. Enough to realize that that was the period the trips to the bottle bank became weekly rather than monthly, what little sex they had turned mostly silent, and every job application Dennis made began to fail at the first fence.

Not that he hadn't fallen for women before, of course. There'd been that pretty girl from Accounts, when he worked at Henderson's. But Bridie had known about that practically from the first day, since he couldn't stop talking about her. And, after that, there'd been his passion for Mrs Hurrell at the Golden Keys – though Dennis would deny to the gates of hell that anything untoward had happened there.

But Liddy. Liddy! Had she been blind, or simply not bothered to look? This shaft of enlightenment – a full five years too late – came so much out of the blue that she might think it was some time-released revenge from powers on high for her own blazing contempt for other people's self-deceptions. But then she'd catch herself. No, stop right there! Don't fall in that old trap of taking the blame. Shove it back where it belongs, onto those who deserve it. Try 'that rat, Dennis', or 'that bitch, my sister'.

But try as Bridie might, it wouldn't take. All week she'd held the rancorous labels up against the two of them, waiting for feelings to kick in. But nothing happened. Nothing. It was as if she'd run aground, as if the years of listening to other, sadder stories had heaped such sandbanks of understanding up around her, her ships of outrage couldn't sail. Who, after all, could blame Liddy? Bridie could recall only too easily the months after Edward's hard birth: Daisy's screams, Liddy's weeping, the foolish mutual decision to let Miles take the contract in Aberdeen. It was no fond enchantress who'd ensnared her husband. Liddy had been a snivelling wreck. And if a man like Dennis strode through her door to fix her roof leak, coax the nappy pins out of her washing-machine drain hose and mend her car, how could she fail to turn to him? He reeked of *family*, for heaven's sake. Safe and dependable. Almost joint stock.

And his betrayal? Even easier to understand. Who wouldn't fall for her? That giddy, sparkling creature, with her bewitching mix of little weaknesses and great enthusiasms. One fat tear down her cheek, and he would gather her into his arms. Easy to see how those cheerful and unthinking brotherly hugs had led to comforts harder to relinquish.

Knock it off, she tried scolding herself. Give up on this unnatural calm. Try hating the two of them just for not telling you. But, somehow, Dennis's secrecy made perfect sense. In a long marriage it is *sauve qui peut*, and if, along with you, there are two vulnerable boys clinging to the liferaft, what is so admirable about offering to let the whole boiling go under, just to come clean about a brief mistake? Bridie had seen enough of family misery after divorce not to believe there was any virtue in spilling the beans simply to salve your own conscience. If anything, she just admired Dennis the more for taking the responsibility to keep his big mouth shut.

And making sure that Liddy shut hers. For she'd have been the problem. Liddy the Great Confessor, Liddy the Must-Come-Clean. Small wonder she believed that any guilt owing to Bridie had long been expiated. For Liddy, staying silent would have been such a penance she would have naturally believed the slate had been cleared. There would be those who'd argue she'd had the better of the deal. After all, borrowing a sister's husband is, for the most part, seen as far more of a sin than letting your bleeding conscience overflow, and spoil someone's dreams. But Bridie knew things didn't work that way. Suddenly they all made sense, those doors closed too hastily, the cries of, 'Bridie, leave it, *please*!' Liddy had made a sacrifice. Dennis had feared the worst, and, with the most to lose, had called the shots. But Liddy would have been certain that, if she had only been allowed to ask, she would have been forgiven. How he must have begged and pleaded with her over the years, not to say anything. How he must have wept and cajoled. How much, how very much, he must have feared Bridie would up and leave him if she knew. How very much, through all those nervous and remorseful years, he must have truly loved her.

And what had the other two done? Sat back and watched. Sat back and watched her husband slipping into the abyss from fear and guilt. The beer crates piling high, her misery growing, Toby and Lance moving out. And they'd said nothing. What a pair of shits! She'd never forgive them. *Never*. One single hint from either one of them, one little word, and she'd have been able to put things straight again between herself and Dennis. She'd have been able to understand what it was eating him, and eating away at what was left of both of them. She could have saved so much. And now the missing anger rose like flood water. Heather, to give her her due, was so selfish, so unthinking, that she had probably let the whole affair slip out of mind almost at once. Bridie had actually been present once when some poor man's wistful, affectionate reference met with such evident lack of comprehension from Heather that it was obvious to everyone standing around that she'd forgotten the two of them had ever been intimate. Someone who couldn't even be bothered to keep track of her own past could probably not be blamed for failing to notice the fall-out from mistakes in other people's. But Stella! Stella was a different matter! Stella would never let anyone's ancient infidelities slip from mind. Oh, she'd stick up for Dennis's reasoning, even lard it with sanctimony. 'No, really, Liddy. He's quite right. Don't say a word. One broken marriage in the family is quite enough.' But, inwardly, she'd be in rapture, like a cat with cream. How many conversations in bad faith can someone clock up over five whole years? Scores? Hundreds? Thousands, even. Bridie could hear herself, even now, tub-thumping as usual. 'I can't *believe* how many wives don't know what's going on!' And Stella's sly, silky echo. 'Can't you, Bridie?' Dropping the last of the knives into the cutlery basket, Bridie slammed up the dishwasher door and leaned on it, breathing heavily. Good thing it wasn't Stella about to walk through that door. Or she would kill her. Positively *kill* her.

'Bridie? Can I come in?'

Bridie looked up from the newspaper she was reading. 'Of course you can come in. Why ever should I keep you out?'

'I don't know.' Frazzled, Heather slung her shoulder bag onto the table, took off her coat and looked round hopefully.

'Coffee?' Bridie offered.

'Angel!' She pulled a chair out from beneath the table and crumpled onto it. 'God, what a morning!' Her eyes narrowed as she looked at her sister. 'And, I have to say, I suspect it's about to get worse, and not better.'

'Problem?' asked Bridie, pouring out a second mug, and sliding it towards her. 'Milk?'

Heather stared. 'Bridie, are we two on the same wavelength, here? I'm looking at a one-week countdown to your never speaking to me again, and you sound totally unruffled.'

Bridie shrugged.

Ignoring the milk jug, Heather started off again. 'I'm here for a reason, Bridie. A horrible reason, I'd better warn you now.' She took a fortifying sip of coffee. 'The thing is, I can't get anywhere with Liddy. Nowhere at all. She won't even talk to me properly. If I mention your name, she just storms off into another room, or says, "I don't want to talk about it, thank you." So I've had to come to my own decision, and now I'm doing what I think is best.' She put the mug back on the table and looked her sister in the eye. 'But it's not easy, and you're not to lose your temper. I don't want you flying off the handle, Brides. You're just to sit and listen. Understood?'

Bridie tried for a moment to look suitably concerned. 'Go on.'

'You're not going to like this, Bridie, really you're not.' Heather took a deep breath, stared at the ceiling and then came out with it. 'The reason Liddy's so wild with you is that you hardly thought twice about hitting her over the head with a rumour that upset them both horribly—'

'Not just me,' Bridie broke in to remind her. 'We all agreed. You even made the call.'

'Yes,' Heather admitted. 'But Stella happened to let slip that she and I had known for quite a while and hadn't felt we had to say anything.'

'Stella let that slip?'

'I'm afraid so.'

Well, well, thought Bridie. Fancy that. 'So that's why Liddy blames me?'

Heather looked more and more uncomfortable. 'Yes, that's why she blames you. But there's something else.'

'Really?' Bridie widened her eyes at her sister. 'Something else?'

'Yes.' Heather squirmed on her chair. 'You see, for years now, Liddy's been—'

'Yes?'

'This is so difficult!'

Bridie didn't help. Heather gathered herself, and rushed into it. 'Look, Liddy thinks you're perfectly happy to risk splitting her and George up with what even you are sure is a rumour – a ghastly mistake. And yet for years now she's been protecting you from something *real*.'

She sat back, waiting for Bridie to ask her, 'What?' But Bridie didn't stir. Heather leaned forward again. 'Bridie, are you listening?'

'Yes, I'm listening.'

Heather carried on. 'For ages now, everyone's been avoiding talking to you about something. We don't even know if you know.' She sighed. 'You're always saying something you've learned from work is that people only keep secrets when others really don't want to hear the truth.'

The stickler for accuracy in Bridie felt obliged to interrupt. 'I don't think that's *quite* how I put it.'

'Perhaps not. But the fact remains, maybe you *do* know . . .' She waited hopefully, but Bridie was still sitting tight. 'And maybe you don't. Anyhow, up until now, there didn't seem any point in saying anything. But now it's different. You're on the verge of riding off into the sunset in a giant sulk, convinced your whole family has deserted you. So it's probably better you're told why Liddy's so outraged, and Stella and I can't budge her.'

Bridie cupped her chin in her hands and leaned over the table. 'Go on, then. What is it I ought to know?'

Heather took refuge in her cooling coffee.

'Biscuit?' Bridie offered sweetly.

'No, thanks.' Heather drummed the sides of her mug with nervous fingers. 'Bridie, I can't believe you never even wondered, when this began, why Dennis didn't just offer to go straight round to Liddy's to try and sort things out.'

'Dennis? No.' Bridie shook her head. 'I can't say I ever wondered that.'

There was a silence.

'Am I going to have to spell this out for you?' Heather asked wearily.

'I think you are,' said Bridie, gathering herself for the performance. She knew she could do it. After all, if there was one thing she'd seen more than enough of over the years, it was clients manufacturing self-righteous outrage. 'Yes, I think you are. And I can tell you why. Because you storm in here after weeks of silence and neglect. Weeks of sheer *cruelty*, in fact, if you choose to be dramatic about it. Yet everything about your manner seems to imply you have some cast-iron excuse for your shitty behaviour. And now, it seems, as one last little torment, I'm supposed to play guessing games.' She thrust her face towards Heather's. 'Well, piss on you, Sister! Piss on you!'

Heather's sheer shock stopped everything for a moment.

Bridie felt sorry for her. But not enough to change her mind and go about things differently. Heather's look of disgust cleared only gradually. Harnessing self-control, she said, 'All right. Here it is, Brides. Liddy and Dennis went to bed together. More than once. Then Miles found out. That's why he left. But, rather than bust up your marriage as well as her own, Liddy's kept quiet about it all these years.' She waited for Bridie to crumple. 'This is all news to you, isn't it? You didn't know.'

She sat, still waiting for the truth of the announcement to filter into Bridie's brain. But Bridie just watched her.

'Think back,' Heather prompted. 'Think.'

'I am thinking,' Bridie told her. And so she was, about a time she'd spent a weekend with friends, and borrowed some sunglasses, coolly thinking, These are nice. I think I'll keep these. And, sure enough, after the last stroll down the lane to where the car was parked, she'd let herself be driven off, fully aware the pretty glasses had been sitting on her nose so long, no-one would even notice. It was the only act of cold calculation in her whole life. Up until now. For why should any of her sisters get away with dealing in truth only when all the effort demanded had to come from someone else? They had all, in their own way, spent the last few months suiting themselves as to what they claimed to believe. Bridie could at least have the pathetic satisfaction of hurling this particular truth back in their faces.

'Heather, I really think you'd better go.'

'Go?' Heather reached over the table towards her sister, who snatched her own hands back at once, and hid them in her lap. 'Bridie, I'm wondering if you've actually taken on board—'

Taken on board! Bridie jeered inwardly. Her sister even talked like a bloody management review! 'Has it sunk in, do you mean?' she asked. 'Yes, it's sunk in. Dennis and Liddy. An affair. That's what you're saying. But I don't believe for a moment that it could possibly be true.' Spite lent her inspiration. 'After all, think of all the things Liddy's always said about people who aren't totally honest in all their relationships. I can't believe for a moment she could be so two-faced. No, really, Heather. It's ridiculous. You're just causing trouble, and you'd better go.'

'For pity's sake, Bridie, why on earth would—'

'Please, Heather. Just leave now.'

'You do realize what you're doing now is the *exact* spit image of—'

'Just *go*, please!'

Heather fell silent. She sat a little longer, no doubt 'reviewing her options', Bridie thought bitterly. Then she stood up. 'All right. I'll leave. You probably need a bit of time to think things through. But I'll be phoning you later.'

'We're having a little bit of trouble with the answer-phone,' Bridie said coolly. 'Not all the messages are getting through.'

Heather opened her mouth to speak and then thought better of it. Bridie passed her her coat.

'Do please give my best regards to Mrs Rigsby.'

Heather looked blank.

'Next Saturday,' Bridie said sweetly.

The penny dropped.

'Bridie,' said Heather, 'this is not like you.'

Bridie smiled blandly. 'People know so very little about one another, really. Until the chips are down. Do you find that?'

She kept the smile up till her sister left.

Sly, careful Stella. Clearly unwilling to be left trailing in the concern-for-Bridie stakes, she showed up early the next day. Standing like a penitent on the doorstep, her head hanging low, she said, 'I feel just terrible. Terrible.'

'No point in bringing your guilt round here,' Bridie said coldly.

'Guilt?' Stella perked up at once. 'I'm not talking about feeling *guilty*.'

Bridie let her in. 'So what is this terrible feeling?' she asked as she watched Stella's eyes flicker round the room as usual, checking on any little changes: things bought, or cleaned, or even simply moved around.

Stella forced her attention back. 'This is awful for everyone, Bridie. We're all suffering.'

'Don't think that's going to let you off the hook.'

Stella stopped struggling to get out of her coat as unease turned to apprehension. 'What do you mean?'

'Just what I say. Mere suffering doesn't exonerate people from what they've done.'

Stella's colour was rising. 'Are you trying to imply—'

Bridie kept on as if her sister hadn't even spoken. 'Though lots of people think it can. Lord knows, I see enough of them. Men who've bashed in their wives' faces.

173

Women who've let their children die of neglect. "Oh, I feel *terrible*!" they say, as if all the leftover pity ought to swivel round to them now. They weep and wail, and tell us how awful things are for them. We can't say anything, of course. It wouldn't be professional. But we can think it. And we do. "All *you've* earned for yourself is *blame*." '

She practically spat the last word in her sister's face. Certain at last that she was the subject of attack, Stella snapped back. 'Listen, I came round here in all good faith—'

'Don't even *start*!' yelled Bridie. 'Don't think I let you in even to take off your coat or look at the sofa! You're not here to lecture me. You're here to *listen*!'

Already, Stella was backing towards the door. But Bridie dived forward to snatch her by the wrists and tug her sharply further into the room. While Stella tried not to stumble, Bridie forced her round, so she was now between her sister and the door. 'Listen to me, Little Miss Spite and Cunning! Don't think I haven't rumbled you. You heard this stupid rumour about George, and you could have just kept quiet about it. In fact, that's far more your style. After all, it's not that often we see *Stella* bothering about what's right or what's best, is it? Haven't you spent your whole life trying to hamper other people in that?' Bridie tightened her grip round her sister's wrists as she launched into cruel imitation. ' "Oh, Bridie, just *leave* it, please!" "Oh, Bridie, don't *say* anything!" "Oh, Bridie, what does it *matter*?" How often have I heard your craven little siren songs? Often enough to know that being straight is not your style.'

'Shut up!' howled Stella. 'Let me go!' In a manoeuvre both of them must have learned back in the same self-defence class, Stella wrenched her wrists sharply down and round, till she was free.

'You're not leaving,' warned Bridie. 'Not till you've heard what I have to say.'

Stella charged at her. Bridie stepped aside and kicked at her sister's shins. Changing tack, Stella turned tail and ran for the kitchen. Bridie rushed after her. 'I know why you told Heather and not me. After all, I'm the bloody social worker, aren't I? I'm the obvious one to tell. But, no. You chose Heather. Presumably because she'd pass it on to me, and then I'd get in trouble telling Liddy, and you'd be the innocent two steps away who had nothing whatever to do with it.'

Stella was rattling the back door knob in a fury. 'I'm not listening to this, Bridie! I'm not listening! Unlock this door! I'm going home!'

'You just hadn't reckoned on Heather's sheer *selfishness*, had you? She didn't even bother to tell me. She probably forgot! Though I'm surprised you didn't see that one coming. After all, when have other people's lives ever meant anything to Heather? Never, in my experience.'

'You've got this all wrong!' Stella was desperately feeling for Bridie's back door key, along the top of the lintel, along the cupboard shelves.

'So after a couple of months you had to give up, and take the risk of telling me yourself.'

Stella turned, white-faced. 'Shut up! Shut up!'

'Shame! Having to dirty your fingers setting fire to your own little gunpowder trail.'

'You're mad! You're crazy!' Stella pushed Bridie, who shoved her back so hard she fell against the door.

'Don't try that again,' warned Bridie. 'Or I might just reach into one of these drawers and get out one of the knives I use for my crappy, untidy cooking!'

She watched with satisfaction as Stella froze.

'You're clever, though,' she went on. 'For someone with such a small mind and such petty concerns, it's really rather impressive. It can't be *brains*, exactly. It must be some sort of primitive instinct to work towards your own best interests all the time. You were banking on my rushing in as usual, trying to do my job. Heather might not give a thought to how badly that would go down with Liddy.' She saw her sister's eyes widen, but Bridie wasn't letting on what she believed, what she didn't. 'But *you* knew, didn't you? You knew *exactly* how she was likely to take it. And ever since then you've been quietly encouraging her in her pathetic self-pity. You've been stoking her misguided outrage.'

'I haven't! I have not!'

'Oh, really? You certainly don't appear to have been doing anything else!'

Stella couldn't help flushing. Bridie peered at her. 'So what was in all this for you? Tell me. I'm curious. What on earth is it that could make it worthwhile to stand by while someone who never did you any harm is slowly destroyed? What are you getting out of this, Stelly? A new "best friend"? The end of feeling on the edge of things? Lady Queen Bee, at last, are you?'

Stella tried cutting through her sister's scorn. 'Bridie,

I'm not even listen—' But Bridie snatched up the breadboard and cracked it down on the counter. The noise rang out, silencing Stella again.

'You are *despicable*,' said Bridie. '*Despicable*.'

And she stepped aside.

'Good day?' Dennis asked her, dumping the groceries on the kitchen table.

Bridie looked up from the sewing basket and broke off humming long enough to say, 'Lovely, thanks,' before going back to her scrabbling. Lifting out two reels of cotton, she said, 'Perfect!' of one, and dropped the other back in the colourful tangle. 'How was yours?'

'Better than lovely,' he declared. 'I got a job.'

'A *job*?'

'Driving!' He lifted a bag of her favourite luxury crisps out of the bag with a half-bottle of champagne. Bridie came over to the table. 'What sort of driving?' she asked him, inspecting the bottle he thrust triumphantly into her hands. '*Brilliant* driving,' he told her. 'Here to the airport and back. On call at any time five days a week, but no more than four trips a day. Uniform. Smart cars.' He lifted a second bottle out of the bag. 'Senior bloody executives, of course,' he explained, just a little forlornly. 'But a job's a job.'

'What's in that other bottle?' Bridie asked.

'Not sure.' He raised the label to the light. 'Sophisticated yet refreshing . . . dum de dum . . . filtered . . . blah, blah . . . hint of loganberry . . . alcohol-free.'

'Really?'

He put the bottle on the table. 'Well,' he said, taking her in his arms. 'It stands to reason, dunnit? You can't have a driving job and be on call, and be a drinker.'

'No,' Bridie said, surrendering. 'You can't have a man with brewer's droop riding the highways.'

Dennis pushed Bridie's hand down onto his zip. 'I expect I'm improving already. Want to check?'

'Not here,' said Bridie.

So they went upstairs.

11

TERENCE WAS HORRIFIED. 'I CAN'T BELIEVE IT, BRIDIE. YOU, OF all people! With the Highfield estate moving into our patch from June, and all the new need proposals. This is *terrible*.'

'I'm sorry,' Bridie said. 'I really am.'

'If I'd had *warning* this was happening . . .'

Bridie sat patiently, having already told him twice that Beth's mother only phoned with the job offer the previous evening.

'I can't believe it,' Terence said again. 'To leave us for house decoration! Honestly!'

'It isn't really decoration,' Bridie said. 'It's more a sort of organizational thing. Apparently, more than three thousand students a year start courses in this city. They all have to live somewhere. Lots of them go into halls of residence, of course. But many more end up in the most horrible flats. Filthy and dangerous. Unsafe locks. Leaking gas appliances. Foetid carpets. Mrs Morani has contracts with some of the college housing offices to keep places up to scratch and make them safe.'

'But why on earth ask *you?*'

'Because I'm *good* at it.' Bridie leaned forward to steal another of Terence's precious biscuits. 'It seems she'd seen Lance's place before I made him fix it up a bit. And then she came again. It was "before and after", I suppose. It did look very different. Anyhow, she seems convinced I'm perfect for the job. "The last thing we're looking for is airy-fairy interior designers," she keeps saying. "This is a feet-on-the-ground job. All you need is common sense." '

'Just what *I* need you for,' Terence said bitterly. He flicked through the double pages of the office yearbook, sighing ever more deeply. 'Oh, God. You're even going to miss the Carlisle Conference!' He looked up. 'I suppose you know this is pure treachery, Bridie. I take it very poorly.'

'I've done my whack,' Bridie defended herself.

'Nevertheless . . .'

'I've said I'm sorry,' Bridie tried to console him. 'I know it's difficult, but it always is. There'd never be a good time. You know that.'

He pushed the yearbook away. 'Oh, I know that.'

'You can punish me,' Bridie said cheerfully. 'I don't mind. I'll be a brave soldier all through my last month. You can give me the Carter family. And the Callaghans. I'll even go and visit Mr Fullerton.'

'Oh, yes! And make sure you never even *think* of coming back!'

'I'm never coming back in any case. I mean it, Terence.'

And she did. For weeks now, she'd been coming in each day to the same petty difficulties and irritations. But everything was different. She had changed. Where once she'd been battening down anguish, now, gradually, all her efforts had become directed towards disguising indifference. Where once she couldn't help seeing slivers of hope, even in desperate situations, now she seemed to walk under the same grey shroud of futility as most of her clients. Always, before, when she walked past the sign on Miss Minto's wall, 'One person can't change the world, but you can change the world for one person', she'd felt her faith renewed, her resolve stiffen. Now, she thought, Sentimental tosh! And it went deeper. There was something else. This was no longer just the common despair of fearing things were too bad for too many people too much of the time ever to make a real difference. Ever since Christmas, the horrible subversive thought had grown and grown that, even if the wand were waved, and ease and contentment were sprinkled on all, they'd be no better off. The world would still be full of awful people making things intolerable for themselves and for others. All Bridie's working life she'd made allowances for spite and selfishness, brutality and ignorance. All of them did. They had to. How else could anyone who was not Christ walk into some of these homes? They soothed one another through the endless meetings. 'It can't be easy, in her circumstances . . .' 'He does very well, considering . . .' 'What can you expect?' What had these been but little wordy gangplanks to make some temporary contact between their own sensible and coping selves and the deprived and the feckless, the unprincipled and the irredeemably bad? Like all the others, Bridie had gone round mouthing the mantra, 'There, but for the grace of God, go I.' But, unlike them, she'd believed it! So, by extension, she had truly thought that if the funding ever fell from heaven, and time and effort were on tap at last, these people would be *different*: kind and good; trying to do the right thing.

So wasn't she the fool? Liddy had money enough to feed her children, energy to take them to the library, time to tuck them in bed at night. And look how she'd behaved. Heather could sit on her expensive couch, drinking her nice wine as she thought things through, and she hadn't done much better. And, as for Stella, she'd put more effort and concern into shunting her precious china nuns along the mantelpiece than she had into playing fair by her sister.

If those in clover can't be good, then no-one can. So what's the point?

Terence tried one last time.

'Bridie, you don't think, at heart, this somehow might be more a family matter?'

Bridie feigned mystification. He spread his hands. 'Clearly, I don't want to pry. Your life's your own, and I can't make you stay, however much we need you. But you've been so upset about your sisters recently. And sometimes it's difficult to—'

'It's not that, honestly, Terence. I'm quite sure.'

'These things can surface in the strangest ways.'

'I realize that.'

'And, in this job, some of us maybe fall back on our families rather more than we should. We sometimes take advantage. So when for some reason they don't come up to scratch, perhaps we're a little hard on them.'

It was excruciating. So, to speed it through, Bridie helped out a bit. 'You mean, like the shoemaker's children always being the worst shod?'

'That sort of thing. Anyhow, it can be important not to expect too much. Give them the benefit of the doubt . . .'

'I'll think about that very seriously, Terence.' Bridie turned to the window, clamping down joy. Her days of giving people the benefit of the doubt were strictly over. The benefit of the doubt was not some favour floating in the air, for anyone to snatch. It must be earned. And, in a family, it was earned by love. And love was not a word, or state of mind. It was a way of treating someone else. The world was stuffed with people glibly claiming of themselves, 'Oh, I love him (or her, or them),' then treating them like utter shit.

'It might just help.'

'Yes, it just might.'

'And if you change your mind—'

'Terence, I won't.'

'No,' Terence said. 'I don't believe you will. I think we've lost you. What an awful *shame.*'

She kept her face grave till she'd left the room. Then they burst out of her: first the broad smile, and then the cheerful hum. If he'd come out behind, he would have tumbled to her secret. He would have guessed it from the spring in her step. What bliss! What joy! What sheer and irreversible relief! How much of her life, her personality even, had been enmeshed in others. Her family had been like some giant, lowering tree, under whose massive shadow no other shoots could ever grow. Out in the sun here, everything was different. Empty weekends were longer, more relaxing. No longer studded by the petty run of sisterly duties ('I really should phone Stella.' 'Oh, God! The chocolate roulades for Liddy's party!' 'Did Heather ring about those tickets? Should I chase her up?'), even the evenings seemed to last for ever. And letting people go was far more fun than hanging in there feeling sorry for them. When you thought, Oh, who *cares?*, what childish chemical was it that flooded instantly through your brain to make your lips twitch and your feet start dancing? When you thought, Let them all *stuff* themselves, why did the underground rill of amusement break out into open laughter? Sometimes in the mirror now, she looked eighteen, as if, along with concern and care, you could toss out wrinkles and sagging. 'Will you forgive me?' Dennis had asked, deep in the dark, before she managed to lay her finger on his lips to silence him for ever. 'Will you forgive *them*?' came the instant echo. And her heart rose. Forgiveness wasn't in it. Forgiveness was what you offered when you'd been wronged. Her sisters, though, had banded together only to set her free. They'd cut her loose, and like some shining helium balloon, she'd risen into warmth and light, and floated off. No strings at last! From time to time she risked a little backward look, testing for pain or resentment or anger, things that she'd seen bind people to one another far longer and more strongly than love. But they were gone now, and she came up clear.

Bringing another worry. Had she somehow been willing everything to work out this way? This glorious, swirling robe of perfect freedom – it fitted her so well that you might think she had been secretly running it up to suit herself over the last few months. Perhaps she was at heart no different from those of her clients who acted astonished when the girlfriend moved out, the boss handed them their cards or the friend stopped phoning. 'I had no idea it was coming!' they all cried. But they could scarcely deny they'd known enough about lovers, employers and friends to get one of whichever it was in the first place. Wouldn't there always be some small suspicion that, for their own hidden purposes, they'd turned that very same knowledge on its head?

And then she thought, Nonsense! I had nothing whatever to do with this. These are the thoughts of some shocked woman from a terrorist attack, who keeps saying guiltily to the officer helping her to the ambulance, 'It must have been my fault. I opened my handbag and the bomb went off', or a child who ill-wishes her best friend with some silly spell, then spends the next few years immured in guilt because the friend gets run over. No, all that I did was take my chance when it was offered me. All that I did was make my escape.

Dennis was waiting for her in the kitchen, perched on the edge of the table, sponging his nice new cap. 'How did it go?'

She swirled round triumphantly. 'I did it! I did it!'

'Really? They didn't mind?'

'Of course they minded. But that wasn't going to stop me.' She caught him peering at her anxiously. 'Oh, come on, Dennis! You've just said yes to a surprise job offer. Why shouldn't I?'

It seemed unarguable. And someone on whom reprieve has fallen like a miraculous shaft of light is mad to argue. And yet Dennis did. 'It worries me, that's why.' And he was having none of her blank look. 'Don't play the idiot, Brides. I'm bound to think there's something strange about all this.'

'Think you've been let off too lightly?'

'Well? Haven't I?'

'What did you want? Screaming fights? Pudding plates flying? Nights of sobbing? Just tell me, and I'll try to oblige.'

Her sarcasm couldn't derail him. He turned her round so he could see her face. 'I'm not trawling for trouble,' he assured her. 'And I'm not ungrateful. It's just that I can't help feeling things can't be sorted out this easily. If they're not bad now, maybe you'll hatch out something worse.'

She brushed his worries aside. 'Oh, Dennis. I did try to hate you, honestly. But I just couldn't, and I can't pretend.'

'Don't even care about me that much?'

She wouldn't smile. 'We made a deal,' she reminded him. 'No recriminations. No looking back. Just you and me, and a fresh start.' Letting the unspoken rider, And you owe me that, lie heavily between them, she turned away to switch on the kettle. 'And I won't be sorry to be rid of the job. They're paying me out for leaving by giving me a whole month of the Carters and the Callaghans. *And* Mr Fullerton.'

'Getting their very last pound of flesh?'

'Pure spite!' said Bridie. And the thought came to her for the first time. Pure spite. Was it possible? Had Stella made the whole thing up? Behind her, Dennis was chuntering on amiably. 'Still, never mind. Soon be gone.' And, 'Yes, soon be gone,' Bridie echoed, knowing right then and there that now the horrid little thought had come to her, she would never be rid of it, no, not ever – not till she knew for sure. One minute she'd been all serenity, free of her baleful sisters, free to start afresh with Dennis and her sons, free, even, to step into a whole new inconsequential world of colour charts and sofa coverings. And then this little thought had burst in her head, scattering its filth everywhere. If there were any truth to it, if Stella really had invented even the rumour about George . . .

Reaching above her head, she fetched down the coffee cups. 'Except,' she said evenly. 'Except that Terence says I might have to do the Carlisle Conference on Friday.'

'Friday? I thought Carlisle was May.'

Bridie kept her back turned. 'No, that's the Hereford workshops. Sarah will take those.' She dropped the tiny seeds of deceit one by one into the freshly tilled ground of his gratitude. 'But, in return, he thinks it's only fair I do Carlisle.' She spooned in the coffee, thinking so fast her fingers turned to thumbs. 'But I could suggest to Miss Minto that she lend us her cottage. We could make a weekend out of it.'

The wail was predictable. 'This is my first week, Bridie! I can't go.'

'Do you reckon?' She didn't dare put any pressure on him, in case, still steeped in gratitude for her forgiveness, he crumpled and let the dubious attractions of Scottish countryside and married sex outweigh the lure of a peaked cap and a glossy Mercedes. 'You're right, of course. And I expect the sessions will drag on till five or six. Or even later.'

'On the other hand, it would get the two of us clear out of town through the wedding . . .'

Hastily, she kicked that ball straight into touch. 'That's right. And you can hear them already, can't you? "The only reason Bridie and Dennis haven't come is that this weekend they happen to be away." ' She turned back to the kettle. 'No, you're quite right. We'll go another time. That'll be better.'

'Still,' he said, coming up behind and squeezing her. 'It is a shame . . .'

'Isn't it?' she said. 'But never mind.' And she said it again when his new mobile phone rang.

On the drive north, Bridie's mood swung from soaring abandon to mean-spirited brooding. The *hills*! she trilled to herself. The *green*! The *light*! And then, as though awe for the glorious and timeless could only keep suspicion at bay for a few moments, how very *convenient* that Stella's little rumour about George just happened to encompass the one weakness on earth that Bridie was unable to ignore. How very *convenient* that all this should come to light just as Mrs Moffat disappeared up to Scotland. And how very *nice* that Stella could step in so neatly to become such good chums with Liddy through all these pick-and-choose wedding plans.

Roots of suspicion, though, run wide and deep. It was *convenient*, when you came to think, that Liddy had found something to get the hump about, so shortly before her remarriage. The *luckiest thing* that she and Bridie were at daggers drawn. Now she could put the whole messy business of her silly affair with Bridie's husband out of mind once and for all, step in the dress that was as close to white as 'cream' could get, and start afresh herself. It was a common enough practice, after all, severing your own old ties, and totally ignoring the claims of other people. Second marriages were notorious for it. 'I'm your new dad now,' a man says to a child who barely knows him, doesn't even like him, and has his own real dad elsewhere. A year or so later, of course, the tune has generally changed. 'If you can't be more civil, perhaps you shouldn't live here!' To keep their fairy-tale constructions alive, these people grew their own variety of briar hedge. 'Oh, no. She's not at all bothered that she doesn't see her father.' 'Yes, I know she's your other granny, dear. But we're a bit too busy to take you now.' Oh, Happy Second Families, built on exclusion and on lies! What a relief for Liddy never to have to spend another afternoon in the company of the man who had caused Miles to leave her, or look at her sister and remember, and feel guilty.

Traffic patrol caught up with Bridie north of Carlisle.

'In a bit of a hurry?'

'Not really.' Not in the mood to offer the usual craven excuses, she said to him carelessly, 'I was just speeding.'

He rolled his eyes as he wrote out the ticket. 'Where are you headed, anyway?'

No need to lie to this man. 'Ecclefechan.'

He peeled the pink slip from the white top copy.

'Twenty minutes,' he warned her. 'Not a second less.'

There were an awful lot of Moffats in Ecclefechan. (It would have been easier, Bridie reflected ruefully, to be looking for a lonely Ecclefechan in Moffat.) But the photographer at the local free paper did finally recall the champion ice-skating granddaughter, Bridie's only real clue, dredged from the memory of some yellowed cutting. And the newsagent round the corner from the talented Fiona pointed out Granny's house without a qualm.

'Bridie! What a surprise!'

And she was in. No third degree. No wondering how Bridie found her. 'Only a few minutes, mind,' Bridie warned. 'Or I'll be late for my meeting.' But how could a few minutes pass without mention of each of her sisters? She was home and dry. Talk of Stella took up the slow boiling of the kettle and the laying of the tea tray. Heather was passed over practically in the pouring of the milk, since Mrs Moffat barely knew her. The good sense of coming 'home' after her husband's sad death took them through to the dregs of the first cup. And then, as Mrs Moffat leaned forward with the teapot, 'But we mustn't forget Lydia. How are things with her?'

Bridie said something about Liddy shaking off a chest cold, and, at the risk of conversational derailment, threw in some invention about Daisy at school.

Then Mrs Moffat came out with it. 'And George?'

Tense as she was, Bridie wasn't imagining anything. The tone had changed. There was an edge to Mrs Moffat's voice. You had to be listening for it, but it was definitely there.

So she was wrong. And, to her own amazement, crestfallen, too. She could actually feel the disappointment flood through her. Clearly she'd driven halfway up the country not out of curiosity, to seek the truth, but to catch Stella out in barefaced, trouble-making lies. How much things with her sisters must have changed! But she had been mistaken. There was the look in Mrs Moffat's eyes, to prove it. George Rigsby: Public Enemy No. 1.

Better be off.

'I haven't seen George for *weeks*,' Bridie said, hoping the sheer dismissiveness of her tone would deter Mrs Moffat from embarking on the story Bridie was now certain had not been invented by Stella. 'In fact, *months*.'

Mrs Moffat packed her response with meaning. 'I'm very glad indeed to hear *that*.'

Oh, dear. Had Bridie sounded too robust? Clearly, she had been taken to mean that Liddy and George had parted. Bridie was just wondering whether to bother to set the record straight when Mrs Moffat went on, 'I'm glad it's over. I never liked to say anything, of course. But . . .'

Her primped mouth spoke volumes. Better sit tight, thought Bridie. It would look odd to make for the door just as the gossip started. Mrs Moffat might think she was leaving from disapproval, and then, uncomfortable at what might filter back to Stella, get on the phone to put some sanitized version of the conversation on record first. Better stay on a little. Maybe even pitch in. 'Wasn't there some rather odd story about him, anyway?'

Bland enough, wouldn't you think? Take it, or leave it. But Mrs Moffat looked appalled. 'Oh, dear! I feel terrible about that, Bridie! Terrible! I simply don't know what to say!' Her worn fingers writhed in her lap. 'Mind you, I did tell Stella in perfect confidence!'

Bridie said cheerfully, ' "Three only keep a secret if two of them are dead," ' hoping this worldly little offering from her mother would encourage Mrs Moffat to feel less guilty. But it didn't work.

'No, but Bridie, dear! Bearing false witness! It's unforgivable. Unforgivable!'

False witness. So not only was the rumour not invented, it also wasn't true. Well, that at least was good news for Daisy and Edward. They'd be safe. It was one last loose end of responsibility from her old life that Bridie could now cut away. 'So all that just turned out to be some horrible mistake.'

'Mistake?' Mrs Moffat's face was reddening more from anger than embarrassment. 'Mistake, indeed! The woman has no shame. Of course it's easy enough to see why someone might be out to blacken the name of the man who's let her down. But making up gossip as nasty as that! Well, it's wicked. Wicked!'

'But that's all it was? Gossip? No truth in it at all? No prosecution? No court case?'

'No, dear. Nothing but spiteful lies.' Mrs Moffat's eyes were glistening. 'And I feel terrible, Bridie. I feel *used*. It's as if my friend Moira and I have been treated like a couple of old sewer pipes to carry filthy untruths, just to cause trouble. I can't help it, Bridie. I feel quite *unclean*.'

Filled with pity, Bridie stepped round the little coffee table and sat beside Mrs Moffat on the sofa. Putting her arms around the trembling shoulders, she said very gently, 'You mustn't blame yourself. It could happen to anyone, honestly.' Her rueful grimace only confirmed her claim. 'It's happened to me.'

'Has it?' Mrs Moffat peered hopefully at Bridie, and then, remembering, said, 'But, dear, you meet some rare people in your line of work, I shouldn't wonder.' She gathered herself bravely. 'It's just that, as Moira says, you don't expect this sort of filth to come out of somewhere as wholesome as Ballenaughie. Mrs Fryer, indeed! Mrs Liar, more like it!' She shook her head fiercely. 'I can't help it, Bridie. I won't forgive the woman. I just don't think it's right to use other people as pawns to spread untruths, even if a man has treated you badly.'

'And had he?' Bridie asked with growing curiosity.

'Well, I think so.' Mrs Moffat patted Bridie's hand to soften the blow of her next words. 'I know you're a very open-minded person, dear, with modern ideas. I expect that you have to be, with your job. But I do think that, even in this day and age, if a man winkles you away from your own lawful wedded husband, then rushes straight off to a new fancy job and spends the next year promising he'll bring you down as soon as he's found somewhere better to live than his horrible grotty lodgings – '

Bridie recalled Liddy's sun-drenched living room, her jewel of a garden, her enchanted bedroom. 'Horrible grotty lodgings?'

' – then just stops phoning.' She gave a disparaging sniff. 'Well, it's certainly not my idea of gentlemanly behaviour.'

'Do you suppose that Liddy *knew*?'

'Only if he told her, dear. I can't see how else. Moira says George and the lady concerned had been very careful to keep the relationship quiet while it suited them. Till all this nastiness started, I don't think either of them wanted it getting back.'

'Getting back?'

'To his wife, dear.'

Now it was Bridie's eyes that were glistening. 'To his *wife*?'

Mrs Moffat corrected herself hastily. 'Well, *ex*-wife now, of course. And who could blame her, what with the looks of the youngest of the Fryer children so obviously favouring—' Catching herself in full flight, she stopped and gave another little sniff. 'No, it's a *midden*, Bridie. A midden of lies and spite. Your sister's well out of it, that's all I can say. And, if you're kind, you won't ever tell her.' Now that she'd got her anger and resentment off her chest, Mrs Moffat seemed determined to put the whole subject behind her. 'Oh, it is such a pleasure to see you, Bridie! Have you time for another wee cup?'

Bridie stood up. 'I really ought to go.'

At the door, Mrs Moffat clutched her arm. 'Bridie, let's not say anything about our little chat.'

'To Stella?'

'To anyone.' Mrs Moffat peered up and down the little street as though the neighbours might be listening. 'You see, with all this unpleasantness, I've made myself a little vow . . .' Again, she checked for eavesdroppers. 'Silly, perhaps. But it's my own little way of trying to deal with what's happened.'

'I understand,' said Bridie. 'You're feeling so raw about this that you don't want anything you've said passing along, in case, later, it turns out not to be true.'

There was a place for 'active listening', then. Stella might not have taken to it kindly, but Mrs Moffat beamed.

'That's right, dear. That's *exactly* how I feel.'

'Don't worry.' Bridie bent to kiss her cheek. 'My beak is buttoned.'

'And if Stella should ask you what—'

'How can I tell her anything?' Bridie interrupted. 'I didn't even get here. What a shame! I came so close.' Airily, she waved a hand towards the little rise between Mrs Moffat's street and the main road. 'Almost past your front door. But what with one thing and another, and the traffic, there simply wasn't time.'

And before Mrs Moffat could start worrying about that, Bridie was gone, knowing two beaks were buttoned, not just one.

Well? Would he risk it? Bridie leaned her arms on the steering wheel and pondered. Scores of people did. Some because they had no way of tracking down their old divorce papers without a deal of trouble, others to hide their less than savoury pasts from general scrutiny. It wasn't hard. All that you had to do was tick the wrong box. (Single, divorced or widowed.) The registrar ordered random checks, but not that often, and you could always argue that your pen had slipped, or you weren't wearing your glasses, or you were a halfwit when it came to forms. It wasn't bigamy, after all. Giving false information might be an offence, but it wasn't as if you weren't entitled to marry. So what had he done, back on that famous pink and silver-tinged morning? When beautiful, joyous Liddy pushed back her tangled hair and said, 'Oh, George! Let's get married!' did he come clean? Perhaps they all knew now, apart from her. Perhaps it was one more little family secret, best kept from meddling, bossy-booted Bridie, in case her tiresome principles ('You can't just not *mention* her, Liddy. She does *exist*') got in the way again.

And perhaps only Liddy knew.

And perhaps she didn't.

Leave it, said Bridie's conscience. Let it lie. It doesn't matter. And how they come to order their affairs is no more your business than how you come to terms with Dennis is any of theirs. So stop it right now, Bridie. Close the book.

And maybe the old Bridie would have been able to hold out. But everything had changed so much. And it's the most human of pleasures, to take the chance of finding out if someone who's done you wrong is even deeper in the mire than you'd dared hope. Her eyes kept falling on the map spread on the seat at her side. Ballengullie, was it? Ballenhauchy? No, there it was, by the crease, a thumb's width from the fold: *Ballenaughie*.

Bridie switched on the engine and slid the car into gear. Was this plain curiosity, she wondered. Or were the gods of malice overhead egging her on, just to make trouble? But as the exhilaration of the chase took hold, a burst of song cut in to match the burst of speed. Bridie's last thought before the bypass was that, with luck, there'd prove to be truth in yet another of her mother's corrosive little sayings.

The more you stir a turd, the more it stinks.

12

'SO WHERE THE HELL *ARE* YOU? ON THE ROAD TO DAMASCUS?'

'No, seriously, Dennis.' She pressed the receiver closer to one ear, and blocked the other against the traffic's roar. 'It's just that I've changed my mind. I've been thinking about it the whole time I've been driving – '

'Brides, you've been thinking about it for *months*.'

' – and, somehow, it all looks different. I want to go.'

The traffic behind her was making a ferocious din. Dennis was silent.

'Hello?'

'They've all been getting at you, have they?'

For a moment, she couldn't think who he meant. 'Who's been getting at me?'

'All those wishy-washy, give-'em-another-chance social workers you've been with all day.'

'Not at all,' Bridie said testily. 'It's much more personal than that.' Searching for a way to convince him, she recalled her few open-hearted moments on

the drive north, alongside the glorious fells. 'It's something to do with the hugeness of things. And eternity.
And not being petty.'

'So now we all have to cancel tomorrow's plans in order
to join you in Christian forgiveness?'

'Cancel what plans?'

'Well, as it happens, I've just invited Tansy and Beth
and the boys round for lunch.'

Round to distract her on the big day, more like. 'Well,
Dennis, you can surely change that to another time. This is
important.'

'And so were we,' he pointed out so softly she could
barely hear. 'For a few weeks.'

Her stomach turned. Take care, she warned herself.
Remember, he who pursues revenge should dig two
graves. (For all its dark air of foreboding, not one of her
mother's.) But when his mobile phone began to purr
and he said hastily, 'Well, it's your funeral. Sorry,
wedding,' her principal feeling was simple relief that
the conversation was over. 'Tell the boys that it's suits,
shirts and nice ties. And make sure they're clear about
the *time*.'

'I have to take this call, Brides.' He hung up. She
stepped out into biting wind. Should she phone back to
stop him before he got in touch with Toby and Lance? Say
she couldn't think what had come over her? But what a
waste that would be. No, Bridie drove on. Rolling south
past Carlisle, she noted the name of a suitable-looking
conference hotel. At Penrith service station she bought
envelopes, and sat at the side of the forecourt filling out

the cheque for the previous day's speeding fine, taking great care not to make any stupid little mistakes that might bring further paperwork down on her head and home. (No point in courting questions about why she should have been on the road, especially that road, when she should have been running some workshop on Family Supervision.) Just south of Lancaster, she remembered to fish Miss Minto's cottage keys out of her pocket and tuck them away in the zippered compartment of her handbag. Were there any receipts still to tear up? ('Didn't they even *feed* you?') And what else? She knew her colleagues wouldn't split on her. She'd seen to that by telling them the only reason she was even taking her last two days' statutory leave was to drive north to buy some special and much-coveted fishing rod for Dennis's birthday. 'Now don't say a word if he phones, or you see him. I've covered my tracks by telling him it's the conference. Don't let me down!'

So that was everything wrapped up – apart from the perfect wedding gift the fates of Ballenaughie had conspired to offer her. That lay on the back seat, still swathed in brown paper. She'd have to have a go at dolling that up properly before tomorrow morning. And herself. What did she have in the closet that had seen a dry-cleaners in living memory? The thin green silk? Stella was right. March was so *undependable*. Would a warm undershirt show?

She was still flapping about with tights and shoes when Dennis finally got home.

'Was that your last run of the evening?'

'I certainly hope so.' He lifted the sleeve of the shirt she'd ironed for him. 'Oh, Bridie! Not this one, *please*. You know I hate it.'

'It is a wedding, Dennis.'

'It was an act of rank betrayal yesterday.' But he was too tired to make an issue of it. And in the morning Bridie was busy fielding the phone calls from the boys. Toby refused to come. He had a date. It had been fixed for ages. Lance was more pliable (except for the business of the nice tie), but still took some persuading. So it was only after Dennis got back from the car wash that he had any real chance to tackle Bridie on her change of mind. 'I just don't understand what's going on. What happened to all your fine principles, all that *outrage*? You said it over and over – if a friend treated you this way, you'd dump them without a thought. Why have you suddenly decided to let them off, simply because they're family?'

'I can't explain it, Dennis.' Though he'd come right up behind her, she refused to turn from the mirror in which she was fighting her unruly hair. 'Except . . .' She flailed about desperately. 'Except that maybe that was the big mistake, judging them as if they were friends. Perhaps the whole point of families is that you have to take what comes.'

He scowled at the hated shirt. 'More's the bloody pity.' But still he wouldn't leave. Clearly, he was planning to stand there and wait for her to come out with some more convincing explanation for her extraordinary change of mind. So, reaching for a hair clasp, she tried again. 'I mean, when it comes down to it, families can't be a matter of pick and choose, can they? Once you bring choice into the business of families, everything's going to fall apart. Who's going to pick the sick and the old and the crazy? They'll have nowhere and no-one.'

He was exasperated. 'Your sisters aren't sick and old and crazy. You said yourself, they're simply selfish and unkind.'

She gave up on the clasp and shook her hair free. It felt a whole lot better, and looked no worse. 'Oh, well,' she said chirpily, 'perhaps the only way to get along with anyone in this life is to wear blinkers.'

He wasn't having it. Turning her round, he cupped her face in his hands and said, 'I'm worried, Bridie. This isn't you. It isn't you at all.'

She smiled seraphically. 'No, really. It's me.'

'Oh, I don't think so.' His fingers tightened round her face. 'In fact, I worry that this is *defeat*. You don't make decisions quickly. You never have. And this big change of mind out of the blue— ' He shook his head, baffled. 'You haven't told them. You haven't even given yourself time to think it through. I think you're trying on some face that isn't yours. Bridie the Saint! But you can't forgive them simply through some act of will. I *know* you, Bridie, and it just won't wash. The minute you see them all smiling at you over the canapés, you're going to regret it. I'm worried you're suddenly going to start burning with rage. Turn turtle. *Explode*.'

She turned her face up to be kissed, hoping her sheer tranquillity and strength of purpose would allay his fears. 'Trust me.'

He studied her carefully before he said, 'I'd really like to, Bridie, but I can't.'

Let him be anxious, if he must. She knew exactly how they would respond, and she was right. From the moment Liddy glanced up and saw the three of them walking in boldly through the wide swing doors of the reception room, she played up the distractions of the occasion, kissing Bridie warmly, then hastily vanishing to sort out Daisy's trailing sash. George followed his bride-to-be's lead, rushing off straight after his series of bear-hugs to some unspecified purpose on the other side of the room. Stella, of course, was little short of fawning, to the extent of letting relief at seeing her sister walk through the door flanked by her family overwhelm any concern about the strain on the catering. 'Oh, Bridie! You'll sit in our row, won't you? I can move other people back. I can nip in right now and shift round a few seating cards.'

'No, no,' said Bridie. 'Dennis is on call. We should sit by the door in case his pesky phone starts.' Ignoring her husband's sharp look, she turned to greet Heather, who was hurrying over, arms outstretched. 'Bridie, you gem! You angel! I knew, when it came to it you wouldn't let your family down!'

'Shall we move through?' Bridie said hastily. Since Dennis's look of blazing scorn made him untouchable, she turned to her son for cover. 'See how smart Lance looks? It'll be his wedding next, I shouldn't wonder.' And, in her agitation, she might even have launched into some desperate description of Tansy's virtues, had not the sudden outpouring from the speakers of the first few bars of one of Liddy's favourite songs sent everyone scurrying to their places. Dennis took Bridie's elbow, and, following her hint, escorted her through the double doors no further than the back row. It wasn't church, but Bridie still felt guilty, as if her bitter thoughts were quite as audible to those around as any of Liddy's and George's clear, solemn responses. Bridie sat watching the brim of Stella's fetching new hat bob up and down, and Heather's freshly mani-cured fingers creep round the back of her collar to check on the fall of its expensive scalloped folds. How she despised her sisters! How could they welcome her with open arms the way they had, with no apology, no self-reproach? It was as if, like George, they truly did believe that people were entitled to choose whichever place they wanted to begin their stories afresh. But it's not fair, it isn't right, to start the accounting always where it suits you, as if the weeks and months of your own cruelties and betrayals have vanished suddenly without trace.

Because they haven't. Open the other person's book, and there you'll see them, black on white. Peel off the layers of offence back to the start of time, but you'll not find a single place at which the two of you can agree, 'This is where it began'. For all that Bridie knew, Stella had suffered years of feeling patronized and slighted. It was quite likely that Heather had reached boiling point a thousand times with Bridie's untiring insistence on family arrangements. And Liddy, almost certainly, had had enough of being forced to hide the truth to oblige her craven brother-in-law and save her sister facing awkward facts. If you were trying to forgive and forget, you could remind yourself over and over of what the four of you had heard so often from on high during the squabbles of childhood. 'Oh, she did that to you, did she? And what, may I ask, were you doing to her the moment before?' If you were trying to forgive, it would be easy. You could decide to call a halt right then and there to all resentment, all ill-will. You could be generous and loving enough to watch your radiant sister turn, first to her new husband, then to all her guests, and you could whisper to yourself the old, old seal on anger: '*Pax.*'

If you were trying to forgive . . .

Now Lance was leaning over Dennis's arm. 'Mum, can I go?'

She raised a delaying finger. 'One more tiny thing . . .'

He wailed at her softly, 'Mum! We had a *deal*. No reception. You said I could go straight after the ceremony.'

'Wait till you hear.' She fished in her bag for her keys. 'You take the car.' His eyes lit up, though, beside her, Dennis was stiffening with disapproval. 'And drop off that big package on the back seat at Giovanni's on your way past.'

'We could leave too, Brides,' Dennis said hopefully.

'We won't stay long,' she assured him. 'Just a few minutes. For form's sake.'

'For form's sake!' But he did his best, rising along with the others and keeping a civil smile on his face as they put on their coats and drifted out. On the way over the square to the restaurant Liddy had booked for her reception, he paid attention only to Daisy and Edward, relinquishing them with reluctance at the door. Inside, he instantly took advantage of the informality of the occasion to steer Bridie well away from what might have passed for a receiving line, had not so many of the guests broken away to fetch drinks from the waiting trays.

'Here, Brides. Have one of their nice poisoned chalices.'

'Ssh, Dennis!'

'Don't you hush me,' he warned. 'I don't know why we're here at all.' Turning his back, he made a point of studying the shelves of bottles ranked behind the bar, affecting not to notice the swarm of in-laws gathering round his wife. In her three-month absence from the family, Neil, too, had cashed in on Stella's growing closeness to Liddy, Bridie noticed. He was the one who took it upon himself to chivvy the waiters, call for a cringe-making 'modicum of hush' for the toasts, and, as Liddy's champagne-fuelled laugh began to tinkle dangerously high, steered her and George across to Bridie's package.

'A present? Now?'

'It's from Bridie and Dennis. I thought it might be nice . . .'

She needed no more telling and moved closer at once. Bridie glanced round for Dennis, but he was nowhere to be seen as Liddy fumbled with the pretty pink envelope and exclaimed with the statutory delight over the card inside.

Neil read it out portentously. ' "Enjoy your wedding — Bridie." And Dennis, of course,' he added off his own bat, presuming that the omission had been some oversight on Bridie's part. As self-appointed master of ceremonies, he flashed her an ingratiating smile on tipsy Liddy's behalf, but Bridie wasn't looking. Her eyes were fixed on George as Liddy struggled merrily with the ribbons, pulled the framed picture from its glossy wrapping, and read the words on the label.

'*Minna in the Sand.*'

And look at that. The name meant nothing to him. Not a flicker. He'd cauterized his past life so well, you almost had to admire him. Minna was not, after all, some name like Margaret, or Ann, where sheer familiarity would deaden any heart-flip within weeks. How many Minnas could you possibly meet as you went through your life? And even if the talk about her parentage was empty gossip, she wasn't easily forgettable. Bridie had trespassed in the shadow of the dividing hedge for only a few minutes, but still she'd seen enough to be convinced that here was a child with a memorably unlimited range of pesky behaviours. The whining and squawking had begun with the very opening of the battered back door. And, in the time it took to hang one single load of washing, her mother must have run through quite a bit of her own ineffectual repertoire. 'Stupid girl! What have I told you about tipping that basket?' 'Well, if you're cold, shut up and go inside!' 'Minna! Stop pulling at that sheet! You'll have it in the mud!' As the inevitable slap fuelled the inevitable howl, Minna's small fists beat in a fury on her mother's legs, and Bridie, altogether absorbed by the sheer disagreeableness of the little tableau, had quite failed to hear the quiet footsteps coming up behind, and was thoroughly startled when, a moment later, she felt a touch on her own arm and heard a voice.

'What on earth do you think you're doing, skulking about in my garden?'

A sticky moment. Even now, the thought of it made Bridie shiver. But who would have thought the woman staring at her with such unblinking suspicion should have become so affable in such a short time? Obviously, the identity card had played its part. (Where children are concerned, there's nothing like an off-the-record visit from the social services to set a neighbour chatting. Everyone, after all, has their doubts about the way other people bring up their offspring.) But once the coffee had been poured, it was probably Bridie's unfeigned admiration for the drawings and paintings strewn around the little house that worked most of the magic. 'Are these *yours*? But they're quite wonderful! Oh, look at this one!' Somehow the deal was struck within the hour. The 'little whispers that have come to our attention' should be discounted. (Mrs Fryer, though undeniably unpleasant, was not a bad mother.) And, from the stack of canvasses just back from exhibition in Traquair, Bridie could purchase *Minna in the Sand*.

And wasn't it a fine likeness? To watch George's face more closely as Liddy lifted the portrait to the light, Bridie slipped forward. It was a pity about the frame – not Liddy's sort of thing at all (no splintered mirror bits, no pastel washes). But then she probably had stacks more at home, much the right size. No, there was no reason to fear that, somewhere in her deliciously cluttered little house, she couldn't find a place to hang the painting – a place where George's eyes could fall on it dozens of times a day.

As they were doing now, with growing horror. It seemed that Mrs Fryer's accomplished next-door neighbour had caught it perfectly, that snivelling, red-eyed, grasping look he must have seen a thousand times over the cot bars, in the high chair – why, in that very sand pit! Not even George had managed to forget that face. Instantly, he turned to scan the groups of inattentive well-wishers, searching for Bridie. She took another step forward, so he could better see her look of gloating challenge. And if the new Bridie had not so successfully frozen her heart against the melting of her icy purposes, she might even have pitied her brand-new brother-in-law in those few moments, such was his anguish and his pain.

'Isn't it *sweet*?' cooed Liddy. 'She looks such a little crosspatch! The colours are marvellous, Bridie. Who's the painter?' She turned the portrait round again. 'Megan McFadden.'

A further tremor running down George's face led Bridie to believe his memory might be coming back fast. Smiling, she turned away, as though embarrassed by the attention being lavished on her gift. Was one more little congratulatory drink in order now? Never again would she lay down a book or walk out of a theatre or cinema unwilling to believe the efforts people would make to pursue their dark, hidden hungers. Now she knew those who'd been thwarted could surrender it all – truth, conscience, habits of kindness, everything – just to get even, just to take revenge. Blanketed by spite, they'd sacrifice all generous impulses to fuel their contrivances, and wipe out their humiliation. And who could blame them? Even the lily-livered who went in for forgiveness must surely dream of fair play, blood for blood. And where was the virtue in holding yourself in check when there was justice to be served? There was a symmetry in revenge that fairness demanded. It was a way of showing these things matter, that principles count, and it will always be important, as Bridie had tried her whole life through, always to do the right thing.

So let every moment of their life together be clouded by this veil of unshared knowledge, just as her own transparent happiness with her sisters had been contaminated the same way. Let George worry. Let him sweat. And let the sheer wearisomeness of keeping guard over his own tongue, and fearing Bridie's, cramp any growing intimacy and shrivel love. The barrier of his silence would lie between the two of them, and she'd feel neither pity nor guilt. They both deserved it. And if she'd had a longer time up there, up at her 'conference' in the north, she might have driven over to meet his former wife, in the hope that she, too, had some accomplished artist right next door, hard up for models. Two portraits would have been an even better present. She could have given them the matching pair.

One of the waiters threaded past and, in the mood for celebration, Bridie reached out again. Liddy moved on to exclaim over some pretty porcelain pomander, another belated gift, and Bridie turned away. Meeting her own eyes in the mirror behind the bar, she raised her glass, still smiling, and drank a toast.

So why did she suddenly notice them? Why, in a room of fifty or more, all chatting merrily, would Bridie suddenly have the sense that everything around her had stilled, as though to let her see, for the first time, two pairs of eyes, busy watching? Well, Stella she could understand. Stella's keen nose would sniff its way into the smallest mystery. But there on the other side, deep in the shadow of the kitchen doorway, stood someone else, someone she'd never thought could stare at her with such dispassion, such impenetrable coolness. She tried to disarm him, raising the glass a second time, as though to say, 'I'm ready now. I only wanted to be here a short while to show there are no hard feelings. Shall we go?'

But Dennis, stern as judgement, never moved.

It was, she thought, quite typical of Stella to feel obliged to come up with some excuse. The two of them stood together on the path, carrying their cardboard trays of leftover canapés, and looking horribly uncomfortable.

'May we come in?'

Bridie couldn't disguise her moment of hesitation. She'd known this visit was a possibility; a likelihood, even. That's one of the reasons she was up so early. But still she hadn't thought it through. She felt a little nervous. Stepping back, she tripped on the box delivered as they were leaving for the wedding the day before. Dennis still hadn't opened it, she noticed, though he'd been up for a good hour before dragging poor wilting Harry out for his walk. Pushing the package aside with her foot, she stepped back to let in her sisters. Heather strode past her into the kitchen to dump her tray on the counter, while Stella hung back, burbling. 'You see, there was far too much left.

And the restaurant just seemed to assume that someone would take it. So we thought that maybe you and Dennis, or the boys . . .'

Failing to sound convincing, even to herself, she let her voice trail away.

Heather turned. 'The real reason we're here', she said, 'is because Stella has something to say to you.'

Stella looked horrified. 'Not *say*, Heather. *Ask*. And it's not just me. We agreed on this, don't forget. That's why we both came.'

Halfway to the kettle, Bridie's hand froze in air. She waited for her sister to hear herself, to recognize in her own words the echo of Bridie's recurrent howls of anguish over the last few months. But Stella stood without a blush, without a single thought.

And she'd been about to offer them coffee! Bridie tucked her hands firmly behind her. Were none of her family in the market for learning *anything* about themselves? Must she push on and on and *on*?

Sensing that, though Bridie had come to the wedding and the reception, no social niceties were going to be offered in return, Heather prompted Stella. 'Well, go on. Get it over with. Ask.'

Stella looked positively hunted. 'It was that gift,' she said at last. 'That painting. I'm worried there's something special about it.'

'Special?'

'Yes. It's not just any old painting, is it?'

'It certainly isn't,' Bridie said cheerfully. 'It was done by a really rather distinguished Border artist I met when I was up there at a conference. That painting had just come back from exhibition in Traquair. I think it may even turn out to be a bit of an investment.'

Heather stirred impatiently. 'I don't think that's what Stella means.'

'Really?' Bridie looked from one sister to the other. 'So what does Stella mean?'

'You know what I'm getting at, Bridie,' Stella said irritably. 'There's something very fishy about that picture.'

Suddenly remembering how infuriating Stella herself had been under cross-examination, Bridie tugged the nearest geranium closer, and started picking off the blighted leaves. There were enough, she noticed, to keep her going all morning. 'Fishy?' she repeated, in her sister's own vague, unhelpful, uncomprehending tones.

'Yes,' Stella snapped. 'You know. *Meaningful*. He saw the picture of that little girl, and he looked really odd. It definitely meant something to him. And so did the name of the artist.'

Bridie kept picking. 'Well, it would.'

'Why?'

'Because George used to be a frequent visitor of someone who lives next door to Megan McFadden. And what with her being quite well known locally, it's more than likely that he learned her name.'

'But how do you *know* all this?'

'She told me when I bought it. You know how things like that come up in conversation. "Oh, I know someone who used to live near there." That sort of thing.' Bridie glanced up from the half-bald geranium to see how all of this was going down. Heather looked half convinced, as if this casual link with some old friend's next-door neighbour might be a perfectly adequate explanation for George's startled response. But Stella knew better. 'It was more than that. It wasn't just surprise. It was *horror*.'

'I thought that, too, you know.' Bridie allowed her air of bland innocence to blossom into an obvious taunt. 'And, frankly, I couldn't help feeling a teensy bit sorry for little Minna.' She watched her sisters stir uneasily at this mere mention of the child so vividly portrayed in the mysterious painting. 'Minna. It's such an odd name, isn't it?' Bridie went on. 'Not at all the sort of choice you'd expect from someone as plain and unassuming as George . . .'

It was Heather who broke the silence. 'Bridie, are you saying that child in the painting is—'

Bridie put up her hand. 'I'm not saying anything. It's all just local talk. But, according to Megan McFadden, it's certainly what the neighbours think.' She turned to Stella, who was looking satisfactorily stupefied, and, keeping her imitation just on the safe side of mockery, added, 'But, honestly, you mustn't say a word! You really mustn't! Keep your beak buttoned, or Megan McFadden will *kill* me!'

Stella went scarlet, but whether with shock or recognition, Bridie couldn't tell. So she pressed on. 'Anyhow, Minna's mother certainly won't want that sort of gossip spreading now that she's trying to get back with her husband.' She picked a couple more leaves off the plant before finishing up virtuously. 'It's easy enough, of course, to try and pick up the pieces of your own marriage when you've already ruined someone else's.'

Again it was Heather who seemed to get there first. 'Are you trying to tell us that George is already *married*?'

'Oh, no!' said Bridie. 'Absolutely not! What a suggestion! No, his divorce is perfectly legal, I'm sure. All signed and sealed.'

It was quite obvious from the look on Heather's face that this news wasn't very much better. 'Oh, Jesus Christ!' she muttered, sinking onto the nearest stool. 'Do you suppose that Liddy *knows*?' She turned to Stella, Bridie saw with satisfaction, glad of the confirmation that Heather understood perfectly well all the sly shifts in intimacy that had been taking place over the last few weeks. Who better to ask than Stella, after all? Stella, who'd been so very quick to take advantage of her sister's exile, and rush in with all her catalogues and pattern books and wedding manuals. Who would know more of what the husband-to-be had told his lover about his former life? What was the point of all those cosy little confabulations about guests and clothes and flowers and seating cards and whatever – what, come to that, the point of all that stubborn disregard for principle, all that betrayal – if, at the end, Stella had no more notion than her sisters of what poor Liddy did and didn't know?

And Stella's anguish was a joy to see as, slowly, slowly, the horrid implications filtered down. Bridie leaned back against the door to the porch, and folded her arms. Go on! she willed. Work it out, Stella! Think it through. Either you haven't been as pally with Liddy as you believe – she didn't tell you this one, did she? That's more than obvious from the look on your face – or, from now on, you can't be. Not with this grisly albatross of knowledge slung round your neck to stink up all your precious girly closeness. Of course, you could always try telling her. If you dare. Just don't forget, you could so easily find yourself cast off into outer darkness, just like me.

Her sister's eyes went bright with unshed tears as it sank in. Here was a secret she could never tell. And never forget. 'How could you *spoil* everything like this?' she whispered, horrified. 'How could you let this *happen*?'

'For heaven's sake!' Bridie spread her hands. 'What on earth could you possibly have expected me to do?'

And out it came. Flawless. Impeccable. And dead on cue. The wail from Stella. 'Bridie, you should have told her!' And immediately after, in tones of outrage from Heather: 'Yes, that would obviously have been the right thing to do.'

Oh, perfect! Perfect! Bridie tipped her head back against the rippled glass, and let the sheer exhilaration of the moment seep through her battered, bartered soul. Her sisters watched, bemused, as the seraphic smile of pure accomplishment spread over her face. The penny dropped as, first chastened Heather, then furious Stella, realized exactly what it was they'd said, and why it sounded so familiar.

'Oh, Christ!' muttered Heather.

Stella's face twisted with rage. 'Bridie, you *bitch*! You utter *cow*!'

Bridie paid no attention. Behind her legs, a tiny gust of icy March wind rattled the cat flap. It whipped up the blackened leaves scattered on the floor and swirled them round, as if the mean little spirits whose help she'd sought were dancing in her triumph.

The cat flap fell back in place. The dead leaves settled. All of the tension of the last few months drained out of Bridie suddenly. The battle won, her legs went jelly-weak. For the first time in weeks, her mind stopped racing. It was over now. All over. She let the healing, soothing warmth of getting even spread through her, moment by moment, and give her peace.

Already, they were at her. 'For God's sake, Bridie! What are we going to do about all this?'

The cheek of it! The unadulterated cheek! Easy enough to want the old Bridie back, with all her schemes and plans for keeping a family going. Had no-one ever told them that corpses don't come back to life, and bonds of love, once carelessly untied, flap in the wind for ever?

'Oh, don't ask me.' Such cool, delicious words! Why had she never, ever said them before? So easy. So gloriously non-committal. If she had known the virtues of detachment from the start, then she, too, could have floated all her life, just like her sisters, on this soft, easy and uncaring cloud. 'No, don't ask me. I'm the last person to tell anyone what to do. Look what happened the last time I tried telling Liddy anything.'

That shut them up. As each stood waiting for the other to start negotiations over again, there was another rattle of the cat flap, with something black and determined poking through.

'What's that?' asked Heather, startled.

'Harry,' said Bridie. 'Back from his walk.'

Remembering Dennis's coldness from the day before, Heather turned to Stella. 'Come on. We'd better go.' Steering her shell-shocked sister towards the door, she mustered the last of her energy for a parting shot. 'At least it's such a horrid painting, she probably won't bother to hang it up.'

'She thinks it's *sweet*,' wailed Stella, spoiling even this. 'She says she's going to hang it on the landing.'

'It'll look nice there,' Bridie called after them, following them into the hall. The front door slammed in her face, and she fell back, helpless with laughter. Leaning against the wall, she let her knees buckle beneath her. Serve them right! They were the ones who started it, after all, this dangerous idea that people don't have to be treated with special effort, special care, simply because they're family. They were the ones to act as though times had changed, and that sort of loyalty was as old-fashioned as cooking from scratch every evening now there are microwave ovens, or watching a programme at the time it's broadcast, instead of recording it for when it's convenient. Well, now they'd learned the hard way, hadn't they? They'd set the times a-changing, but she'd changed too. And they'd be sorrier than she would. What had she ever got out of it, anyway? She'd tried to fill the gap left by the death of their mother, and all her reward had been was constant bloody arrangements, some massive phone bills, and a husband so neglected his arm kept reaching in the fridge. No, she'd be glad to be rid of them. She wouldn't have to think about them any more. Their ups and downs could not affect her life. She'd be as happy to see the back of them as the last of all the losers from work. Like Dennis and the Marleys, she'd meet them only when it suited her – weddings and funerals – and, apart from that, they'd keep their distance (just like a *proper* family). No doubt the memories would surface from time to time, set off in unguarded moments by something typical: a laugh like Liddy's over a room at a party; a line of gin and tonics in a theatre bar; lawns mown in perfect stripes. But she would be distracted in a moment. They'd only bring the briefest whisper of regret.

Dennis was in the doorway. 'What are you doing, Bridie? Laughing? Or crying?'

She couldn't say because she couldn't tell. Suddenly nervous, she started scrabbling at the package on the floor. 'Oh, look. It's that bit for the vacuum cleaner, come at last. Let's hope that this one fits. It took them long enough. I shall be furious if—'

Kneeling in front of her, he prised the stupid, bendy, plastic hose out of her grip, and laid it on the floor. 'Bridie, there's something that I have to say to you.'

'No!' Bridie tried to stop him. 'I can't talk now, Dennis. It's all been far too much.' She didn't dare look up, knowing she'd see exactly what she'd seen the night before, when she'd reached out for him, and he'd turned away, embarrassed. 'Can't we just put all this behind us? Remember what I said to Heather, about us probably going off to France this weekend? Well, let's just drop everything, and do it.' She was gabbling now, in her determination to stop him saying what she knew would come. 'Let's go to Deaulort. You really liked it there. You said so. Do you remember?'

'Actually,' he said, 'I was just thinking of moving in with Lance and Toby for a few days.' He patted her hand to comfort her. 'Just to think about things a little.'

So it was out. She might as well look up and meet his eyes. 'With Lance and Toby?'

'Just for a while.' He took the end of the extension tube and blew across it. The most forlorn note, like a ship leaving harbour, like a cry of loss, swelled through the tiny hall. Panicking automatically, Bridie started to beg him. 'Dennis, please don't go!' But the professional touchstone sprang to mind. 'What people get is, all too often, what they want.' She knew now, only too well, that it was true of all three of her sisters. But was it also true of her, right down the line?

As far as this?

No! Don't think about that now! Right now the only important thing was not to let him slip away. Not till she was certain, anyway. Not till she knew.

Plaintively, she said, 'You can't walk out on me, Dennis. Not just like that. It isn't fair. After all, I forgave *you*.'

He blew the note again. 'Oh, Bridie. That was so different. That was only about something I did. This is about what you've become.'

She sat in the dumbest misery. She couldn't argue. He was right. Within a matter of weeks, she'd changed from being the woman he had always loved into someone as sly and calculating as Stella, as self-regarding as Liddy, as unfeeling as Heather. He had been watching her from across rooms, and listening at cat flaps, and he had understood that she had sold her soul. He'd seen her fierce and predatory desires for what they were. And they repelled him.

Her mother's cynical advice rang in her head. The wise man tries sitting on the hole in his carpet. Could it be true? Her fingers scrabbled in the shreds of packaging spilled on the floor. 'Please, Dennis. Can't we try again? You at least owe me that.'

Her heart seized with the pain of seeing from his face that he wished that she hadn't asked. But now at least she knew that she'd be able to reel him back with tears and promises, and memories of their long-shared past. For he was, after all, a decent man, and would, like her, want to be absolutely certain he wasn't making a mistake.

He took her hand. 'Oh, Bridie. Bridie.'

She let the tears roll, not even sure if they were real or fake. That part of her that had the gift of pity and of love was long gone now. She hardly knew herself. She only knew that, like the stupid extension tube lying between them, what would link them now was the shadow of secrets. His, that he couldn't love her any longer. And Bridie's. That it had all been worth it. She didn't care.

THE END

KISS AND KIN
Angela Lambert

'A HIGHLY READABLE NOVEL ABOUT LOVE AND LOSS'
Express on Sunday

Life for the newly widowed Harriet Capel is not
expected to hold any surprises. It will be spent watching
over the vicissitudes of her children's marriages and
relationships, and looking after the grandchildren. That
is, until she sees Oliver Gaunt again. He is her daughter-
in-law's father. The relationship between the parents-in
law has always been difficult since their children's
wedding day and few words have been spoken. When
they meet, they do not at first recognise one another, but
the physical attraction between them is powerful and
instantaneous. As their love affair gathers intensity and
pace, so do its consequences for the family as a whole.

In *Kiss and Kin*, two generations walk a dangerous
tightrope between fidelity and parenthood, each guarding
past and present secrets, the revelation of which, in the
white heat of passion, may destroy the carefully erected
boundaries of tradition and propriety.

'A WRY LOOK AT LOVE AFTER THE MENOPAUSE . . .
CANDID AND ENTERTAINING'
Mail on Sunday

'SPIRITED, SHREWD AND STYLISH'
The Scotsman

0 552 99736 6

BLACK SWAN

A SELECTED LIST OF FINE WRITING
AVAILABLE FROM BLACK SWAN

99313 1	OF LOVE AND SHADOWS	Isabel Allende	£6.99
99766 8	EVERY GOOD GIRL	Judy Astley	£6.99
99619 X	HUMAN CROQUET	Kate Atkinson	£6.99
99687 4	THE PURVEYOR OF ENCHANTMENT	Marika Cobbold	£6.99
99670 X	THE MISTRESS OF SPICES	Chitra Banerjee Divakruni	£6.99
99587 8	LIKE WATER FOR CHOCOLATE	Laura Esquivel	£6.99
99755 2	WINGS OF THE MORNING	Elizabeth Falconer	£6.99
99795 1	LIAR BIRDS	Lucy Fitzgerald	£6.99
99721 8	BEFORE WOMEN HAD WINGS	Connie May Fowler	£6.99
99760 9	THE DRESS CIRCLE	Laurie Graham	£6.99
99774 9	THE CUCKOO'S PARTING CRY	Anthea Halliwell	£5.99
99681 5	A MAP OF THE WORLD	Jane Hamilton	£6.99
99778 1	A PATCH OF GREEN WATER	Karen Hayes	£6.99
99757 9	DANCE WITH A POOR MAN'S DAUGHTER	Pamela Jooste	£6.99
99736 6	KISS AND KIN	Angela Lambert	£6.99
99771 4	MALLINGFORD	Alison Love	£6.99
99688 2	HOLY ASPIC	Joan Marysmith	£6.99
99733 1	MR BRIGHTLY'S EVENING OFF	Kathleen Rowntree	£6.99
99781 1	WRITING ON THE WATER	Jane Slavin	£6.99
99753 6	AN ACCIDENTAL LIFE	Titia Sutherland	£6.99
99700 5	NEXT OF KIN	Joanna Trollope	£6.99
99720 X	THE SERPENTINE CAVE	Jill Paton Walsh	£6.99
99673 4	DINA'S BOOK	Herbjørg Wassmo	£6.99
99723 4	PART OF THE FURNITURE	Mary Wesley	£6.99
99761 7	THE GATECRASHER	Madeleine Wickham	£6.99
99591 6	A MISLAID MAGIC	Joyce Windsor	£6.99